The Ouija Board Killer
An autobiographical novel

Donald Macnow

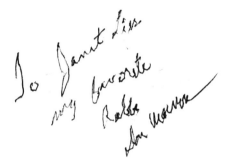

Dedication

To Georgie, my wife and life partner in this
incarnation and for all eternity.

Acknowledgements

Thanks to Leona DelValle, Jay Goldstein and Peter
Valenze for their help in proofreading the
manuscript and for their helpful suggestions.

We have no right to assume that any physical laws exist, or if they have existed up until now, that they will continue to exist in a similar manner in the future.
Max Planck (b.1858- d.1947) - founder of the quantum theory for which he received the Nobel Prize in Physics.

**Hell is empty,
And all the devils are here.**
William Shakespeare, *The Tempest.*

On March 16, 2000 I learned that the odds for my being alive in the year 2005 were only one in seven.

March 16th was the day I received the results of the CAT scan. It indicated lung cancer; the years of smoking had caught up with me. However, today, eleven years after the initial diagnosis I am alive and healthy thanks to a spirit from another dimension, a spirit that entered my body through the Ouija Board

The book, *The Ouija Board Killer*, is an account of many of my paranormal experiences, and woven into a fictional novel of possession, madness and murder, a Dr. Jekyll and Mr. Hyde story of a dual personality, one good and one evil.

Part 1 - New York

Tuesday 1:00 AM

The little red LED lights blink on and off in a rapid sequential motion, first illuminating the bottom of the screen, then jumping to the top, contracting one moment and expanding the next. The lights spell out, "Goodbye World". Goodbye World is on the marquee of the pinball machine I see in my mind's eye as I lie in bed staring up at the blank ceiling. "Try Your Luck" the machine screams at me. See how long you can keep the little chromium ball in play. Pull back on the spring-loaded plunger. Let it go and watch the ball zoom up the track and fall into the maze of bumpers. See the ball bounce back and forth through the playing field. Sometimes it slides sideways to crash into another bumper and sometimes it soars right up to the start of the playing field and you let out a sigh of relief because you know the game will last a little longer. "Ding-ding" it shouts as a kaleidoscope of lights flash and wink. Get a high enough score and you get a free game and a chance to play a little while longer. But this pinball machine, this cursed contraption in my head does not have bumpers scoring in numbers of 10,000 or 50,000 or even the illusive "free game". Instead, they have lights that indicated minutes, hours, days and months, and there is no jackpot to get a free game. Neither does the pinball machine have a set of flippers as does the machine in the arcade. There are no buttons I can push to send the little ball back up the playing field to get a few more minutes of play and to tally up a higher score. So even though I try to push and jostle the machine, always mindful of the feared "tilt" which ends the game on the spot, the ball keeps falling towards the accursed black hole that turns out the lights and ends the game.

Next to me my wife Susan sleeps peacefully. I haven't told her the CT scan results, nor have I mentioned the compelling pinball machine on the bedroom ceiling. My mood is one of despair, and I am tempted to wake her, tell all, and have her share my misery. Instead, I decide to keep my secret a little while longer. Let her rest and enjoy a few more good days before I set the fuse on our time bomb.

It's not my nature to be moody for very long though, and I begin to have a more positive attitude. My friends think me a clown, always happy, always cheerful, and I play the part well not wanting to shatter the image they have of me. And since I have always portrayed myself as a positive person without a care in the world I actually became that person. It's the Pollyanna effect.

This morning when I found out that the scan confirmed the x-ray taken a week earlier, and that I more than likely had lung cancer I was devastated. Well perhaps the word, "devastated" is a bit too overstated, after all is said and done the scan simply verified the earlier diagnosis, so I had ample time to digest the potentially bad news, and come to terms with it. But you can't cry forever. Life goes on and I will just have to make the best of what is left of my days. So like Scarlet O'Hara, standing erect and proud looking west at the setting sun as it casts long shadows over the desolated fields of Tara, I say to myself the words she uttered, "I'll worry about it tomorrow."

Another hour passes. I go through periods of acceptance and denial, good moods and bad, and while I'm still awake staring at the ceiling, my focus shifts to more urgent matters, like: what can I do about the doctor's report? Is this really the end or can I squeeze a few more months, or even better, a few more years out of my life? Surely this can't be the end. My Aunt Ida, the psychic aunt once told me I would have a long and happy life. She told me this over sixty years ago, and in the 1950s I guess a long life was about sixty-five, so I can't hold much stock in that predication. But she was right about the "happy life" part of the palm read. Life has been good. So good in fact that I hate to see it end. And if my life does end what comes next? I believe in reincarnation and my one worry is that I will come back as a blind beggar on the streets of Mumbai. No, I wouldn't want that. Maybe if I accepted Jesus I can be saved and end up in heaven. It's not my idea of a fun eternity, but it sure as hell beats a bevy of other incarnations. So what's a person to do? How does one extend their days? For starters, I suppose I'll have to give up smoking. After all, that's what got me into this mess. Traditional medicine may provide a few more months and maybe even a few years but traditional protocols are not going to help in the long run. I suppose I'll have to endure whatever the doctors suggest. I'll let them pump chemo through my veins. I'll sit under the debilitating x-ray machine that destroys your red blood cells with radiation. I'll do whatever is necessary to extend my life for a little longer, but in the end it's going to be something extraordinary that will save my life. It's either that or suicide, the ultimate solution.

Tomorrow I'll start formulating a plan, one for survival and one to end the pain in my own time and place. I'll look into alternative medicine. Perhaps prayer will help. I really don't think so, but what the hell, it's worth a try. And there may be other esoteric solutions. I'd make a pact with the Devil if I have to. Perhaps I'll get a gun and end it quickly, but it will have to be kept hidden from Susan. This will be another one of my little secrets. If Susan ever found a gun in the house she wouldn't even mention it to me. She would just render it inoperable and drop it into the nearest garbage can. I actually admire her gumption. She seldom argues with me and I can honestly say we never had a real fight in our long marriage. Susan just does what she wants to do, and after the deed is done it's too late to argue about it. But I can also circumvent her possible actions. I used to be a boy scout, and I never forgot their motto - "Be Prepared".

Thursday

I still haven't told Susan the results of the scan, and I still haven't stopped smoking. But I have made some progress. I came to a conclusion on how best to end my life if the cancer is determined to be fatal. I had considered jumping off a roof, but I'm afraid of heights, and it's a messy way to go. Overdosing on pills doesn't always work, nor does sitting in your car in an enclosed garage with the engine running. Often someone finds you at the point where you are still alive but have suffered brain damage, and subsequently vegetate in an irreversible coma for the next twenty years. So all options considered, a gun is the best choice, and I'll have to get it right away before I become too incapacitated to drive to a gun shop.

It might be a bit premature to prepare for the end right now, but I had a friend who was terminally ill, and felt the same way I do. Unfortunately he waited a little too long. He procrastinated, saying, "I'll tend to it tomorrow". However his illness progressed so rapidly and was so debilitating that he was never able to leave his house to procure a weapon that would end his life, his suffering. And he did suffer, but not before exhausting all his savings. That is something I don't want to happen to me. A person works all his life to build a nest egg for retirement, or to leave an estate for his children so they can have a better life, or to fund his grandchildren's education.

But in my friend's case neither happened. He died penniless. The doctors and the nursing home got it all. He left this world as he entered it, bare assed naked. His legacy was only fond memories in the minds of those he left behind.

Friday

The morning started out as any other. Well actually it didn't. At least for me it didn't. And I don't suppose it ever will until my life resumes its dull routine. The sun came up on schedule, and the bright yellow leaves of the maple trees continued to fall, covering the earth as they always do in the first weeks of November. The neighborhood kids caught the yellow school bus, and little Joey had to run to catch it as he often did. Outwardly life moved on as it always does in my suburban village of Locust Valley, and I hope I can say that a year or two from now. However, I don't think it will go on for me unless I personally do something about the situation. "There must be something I could do to save my life", I thought, and I was determined to somehow find a way to extend whatever little time I had left.

After much introspective thinking I finally came up with a viable plan and it was to supplement traditional medications with a few unconventional treatments and therapies as well. I would not rule out anything. But first I had to get a gun in case all else failed.

When I finished breakfast I went into my home office, locked the door, and turned on the computer to search the web for a gunsmith within driving distance of my home. I make a lot of internet purchases but a gun is one item you can't buy online in New York State, and I am not acquainted with any shady characters trafficking in illegal unregistered weapons. Besides, I would need some hands on help with the selection of a firearm. I didn't know the first thing about weapons of any sort other than the M-1 carbine fired just once on the shooting range in boot camp while in the service of our country.

The computer search turned up a few gun shops, the nearest one being in the town of Jackson, and while I hate driving on the expressway in rush hour traffic I gritted my teeth and drove the forty-five minutes to the store. Driving to Jackson is like leaving Shangri La in the springtime when the flowers are in bloom and going to Watts in the first few days after the riots. Racehorses graze in lush paddocks, and homeowners vie to get their homes featured in *Better Homes and Gardens* magazine in my Shangri-La, while Jackson is like Rome after being sacked by the Vandals.

***

When I arrived at Jackson it was shocking to see how blighted the town had become. Half the stores had either been razed to the ground or boarded up. The ones still in business have security shutters that roll down over the doorway at night after business hours, and iron bars covering the windows allowing light to pass through but preventing all but the smallest animals from passing through. The streets are littered with rubbish, and the few people you see in public are for the most part homeless vagrants huddled in the doorways of vacant buildings, or dope pushers standing on street corners waiting for their customers. The town appeared to be a movie setting in an apocalyptic futuristic film with the few people left alive walking the streets in slow zombie like movements, reaching out with extended arms to vehicles passing through the town, and the drivers speeding on hoping to escape the terrifying walking dead.

The gun shop was easy to find. It was on Main Street, and fortunately there was a fenced in parking lot with direct access to the store. Good thing too, because I certainly would not have left my BMW on the street, and risk loosing a set of wheels.

When I entered the shop it was like walking into an arsenal, except for the graphic pictures on the walls. A military arsenal would never approve of such un-politically correct images as displayed in the shop. The walls were plastered with ads that would give a serial killer an orgasm. Brave men dressed in the finest clean and pressed hunting outfits aimed their riffles at several geese flying overhead. Another poster showed a giant grisly bear standing on his hind legs with menacing teeth bared, waiting to be killed by a hunter standing before him. The most upsetting graphic was a framed picture of a deer; its rear legs bound and hung on a hook, the animal upside down, the antlers brushing the ground. Standing beside the stag stood two men, guns in hand, smiling proudly. All in all, the visual images of senseless killing turned my stomach.

There were guns everywhere, handguns of all sorts, AK-47s, machine guns, assault rifles, big guns and small ones, you name it and it was available for sale. The staff consisted of two sales clerks manning the store, one was a middle aged man who seemed normal enough except for his slow foot dragging shuffle as he moved about the establishment. His face was sallow and drawn, his eyes sad and tired. I imagined him never leaving the building fearing for his life if he left the fortress. The second salesman was a little gnome with a holstered western style six-shooter, the gun visible so everyone could see he was a tough dude. He looked like he was ready for a fight and I'm sure he wished a riot would break out on the street so he might finally get a chance to shoot a live person. I viewed the little guy with loathing and disgust. If there is one thing I can't tolerate its people who kill defenseless animals. I hate guns, and I never would be in the store except it was an absolute necessity to own a weapon, the ultimate solution. If nothing cures me I will go into the woods with a thermos of cold martinis, sit on a rock, have a few drinks to steel my nerves, and do what Ernest Hemmingway did, blow my brains out.

The salesman left his task at hand, the cleaning of a semi-automatic weapon, and approached me. As he closed the distance between us I thought, "What the hell am I doing here? Is it too late to change my mind?" The uncertainty must have shown on my face because the salesman had the look of a Cheshire cat ready to devour a mouse, his breakfast meal. The gnome knew he had a sale if he pushed hard enough.

The little guy introduced himself with an air of arrogance. He compensated for his size with a super ego and inflated his chest with pride while bragging about his hunting prowess. He claimed to have personally shot every breed of wild, and on occasion a not so wild animal in the Northeast, and he could give me a firsthand assessment of every gun in the shop. Was I supposed to be impressed? I would be embarrassed to admit I killed helpless creatures. But I kept quiet and did not reveal my displeasure. After all, nobody forced me into the store. I came there of my own free will.

After regaining my composure, and resolve, I examined an impressive array of weapons. There were a few small caliber guns for target shooting and a whole lot of automatic machine guns capable of taking out a squad of soldiers or a gang of drug dealers with just a single clip of ammunition. Not knowing anything about guns or local laws related to owning a weapon I thought a basic revolver would suit me best, but I immediately rejected that choice when the salesman told me there would be a stack of paperwork to fill out in addition to a background screening and fingerprinting by the local police, and a hefty annual permit fee. The expense and time it took to get a hand gun didn't seem to be a good solution for a one time use.

I tried out a few rifles but their barrels were too long for me to reach the trigger and still have the muzzle pointed at my head. If I had only wanted to remove a few toes a rifle would have been the perfect weapon.

After considering a variety of weapons I told the salesman I wanted something inexpensive that might be used to scare off an intruder bent on burglarizing our home. Of course I was lying. I would never reveal the true purpose of the gun. He finally directed me to the weapon of his choice. It looked like a sawed off shotgun, something Clyde Barrow might have used in his rampage through the Midwest with his girlfriend Bonnie. "This is the perfect solution for effective home defense", the salesman said. "If someone breaks in, and if you can get close to the burglar, this gun will cut him in half." Yeah that's just what I needed - a bisected dead guy lying in the foyer. He also said "You don't want to wound him. It's got to be a clean kill because if he survives he for sure is going to sue you". The gnome was right of course. After all, a gun is for killing not just for wounding.

***

I once had a friend whose teen-age daughter was so distraught over her boyfriend leaving her she attempted to commit suicide. Unfortunately the only weapon my friend had in his house was a .22 caliber target pistol, very lightweight and not very powerful. When his daughter tried to do the deed her hand trembled to such an extent she missed a clean shot, and the bullet did not enter her brain but did manage to pass through both eye sockets blinding her for life. In time she got over the failed romance but the loss of her sight was forever. There is a moral here somewhere, but I'm not sure what it is. However, I do know I would have only one chance to end my life, so I placed an order for a Stevens pump action short barrel home defense weapon, a 12 gauge meat grinder shotgun.

***

Feeling satisfied that I had taken control of my fate, or at least the first step in determining my own destiny I drove home in time for lunch. However, I did not go straight home. I made a stop at the local supermarket to stock up on some foods I had not eaten in years, foods that were as forbidden in our home as the proverbial apple in the Garden of Eden. Pork, well marbled beef, processed sandwich meat, rich whole milk, real butter and a few other foods designed to shorten your lifespan were no longer off limits, or if I can use a bad pun -- off the table. I figured there was no sense in eating healthy if I only had a short time to live so when I returned home I left the unpalatable bland food in the fridge and made a pepperoni and cheese sandwich, a side of potato salad floating in real mayo, and to end a good meal, topped it off with a king sized cigarette. I know it's crazy to think this way since I still had hope that I might live another twenty years. But in another vein it's great not to have to worry about all the unhealthy foods that might eventually kill you. As I said earlier, it's the Pollyanna effect.

After lunch I went upstairs and locked myself in my office, my private space. It has a sign on the door that says, "Do not enter without express permission of the boss." So far no one has challenged the sign even though Susan is the real boss of the house. This is my domain and everyone respects my privacy. I'm sure Susan thinks I'm hording a library of porn movies, and she is OK with that. But the truth is -- it is just my home inside my house.

The office consists of a desk cluttered with stacks of notes and papers that should be looked at, and sorted out as to garbage, and what is important. Actually Susan gets all the important stuff or else the mortgage, tax bills, phone bills and all that "stuff" would never be paid, so I suppose you can say my desk is a repository for garbage. Aside from my desk there is a six tier bookshelf stacked with books, some of which I read many years ago, and others that will never be read. My one bit of luxury is a high backed leather chair facing the computer desk. Almost everything except the desktop computer and the nice soft chair can be tossed into the trashcan for all I care. It's the computer I cannot do without, especially now. It may hold the only answer for my survival. I'm planning on surfing the Internet and hopefully retrieving un-published medical breakthroughs, or holistic cures, or esoteric information that could be used to save my life.

I went online and researched the latest medical advances. There weren't any that pertained to my condition. Oh, there were some clinical trials going on but not for me. I was too old, or there were other conditions that had to be met, and I could not meet them. There was several "for profit" websites which I am quite certain are scams. The websites are for people who are so desperate that they will believe anything, and they will pay anyone, a doctor, a TV Evangelist, a physical therapist, anyone at all if they promise a cure whether or not the cure is effective or can be documented. The clients of those mercenary bastards will exhaust all of their savings if there is even the slightest degree of hope. I hope I never get that desperate. It must be terrifying to fear death so much.

There was also information promoting overseas clinics that often sounded credible and legitimate. The word, "Clinic" lends some credibility to the establishment, but most of them are just another scam. The computer monitor shows concerned practitioners wearing white sterile gowns working in modern hospital looking settings and it is assumed they are medical professionals, but they are only actors. One clinic in Mexico featured injections of monkey fetuses for a cancer cure.   Another clinic took the shotgun approach filling your body with organic concoctions that are injected, ingested, or placed in orifices you don't want to talk about. My favorite off the wall cure was the one that had you drink two gallons of silver-iodide water in a 24 hour period, and to repeat it every day for two weeks. You can bet they have a disclaimer for that cure. No one can drink that much water in one day.

Holistic remedies, topical salves, and cures based on herbs, roots and other foods are a waste of time and money except for the growers and processors of the edibles. Several years ago eating almonds were in vogue as a means of both preventing and curing cancer. I wonder who promoted that cure; think maybe the almond growers association. Deep down inside I don't believe healthy foods mean a damn thing in assuring longevity. Susan feeds me rabbit food and what did it get me, nothing, except maybe a shorter lifespan. I'd rather follow my mom's diet. She, being raised by parents who emigrated from Russia was brought up on a Jewish peasant's diet, which was fatty meats, lots of salt, potatoes and very little veggies. She lived to be 92. When it comes to food my motto is, "eat and enjoy". Beside, what's in vogue today may not be so tomorrow. Recently it was announced that milk is bad for you and coffee good. I remember my high school football coach giving the players salt pills after a hard workout. If a coach tried that today he would be looking for a new job.

I researched the promise of miraculous cures through prayer. There are members of the First Church of Christ, Scientist who never seek medical help. I thought perhaps there was something to their beliefs. But I found out that when the going gets tough, the tough get going and "the going" is to a doctor. Those who don't seek medical help often die, but then the church says, "It was Gods will". It's a win-win situation for the church. I looked into less well-known religions ranging from Scientology to the more obscure ones such as Kabbalah to see if any of them might provide a cure. That was really a waste of time. Miraculous cures are a one in a million shot, and you have to believe in their dogma, and I don't, so religion holds no answers for me. As hard as I try I cannot believe in any organized religion, although there are a few elements of many religions I could embrace. For example, I could embrace Buddhism if they eliminated some of the gods, deities, and rituals, and only kept meditation, reincarnation and karma.

If someone had a witches brew, a large cast iron cauldron boiling and bubbling over an open flame, and stirred in a chunk of Buddhism, a little dash of Hinduism and spiced it up with some metaphysical, and paranormal tenets and doctrines, then maybe I could join a religion that makes sense.

I also surfed up some mystical nonsense, most of which was pure hyperbole. But there was some interesting information on the Internet that was also contained in the dusty books on my bookcase, only updated with a new twist or two. Years earlier, simply out of curiosity I had read the collections of esoteric books stacked high in my library, and had delved into the metaphysical sciences for pure amusement. I referred to the paranormal at the time as, "things that go bump in the night" regardless of whether they were poltergeists, mystics or frauds. But I never took the information I read very seriously. Now my life may be riding on the occult. It's not party games anymore. It may be wishful thinking, and I may be grabbing at straws, but I have now come to believe that perhaps the information gleaned from books and online might prove helpful, so I browsed through the books again, and seriously considered what made sense and what did not.

The old dog-eared books reaffirmed my belief that anything concerned with religion was out. There were no easy answers or instantaneous solutions for my problem. Recent clinical studies indicated prayer might help effect a cure. Unlikely as it seems there is evidence to the little known fact that prayer does work, but only if it's a concerted effort with a church full of people praying for an individual. Where was I going to find dozens of parishioners? I don't even have a religious affiliation.

Traditional medicine, chemo, and radiation will forestall the inevitable, and I will go that route but only up to a point. But I won't let the doctors turn me into a vegetable slowly rotting away in an uncomfortable hospital bed with tubes and needles puncturing every vein. I'll have the shotgun as a final solution if it comes to that. This leaves me with only one alternative, and the alternative is to find a cure through very unconventional means. I will have to tap into the occult.

***

Later that evening Susan and I did what we usually do after dinner, we watched TV, a forgettable movie, and at ten o'clock took a break. We sat in bed, clicked the remote to "pause" for fifteen minutes and consumed a huge slice of chocolate cake with a glass of milk to wash it down, a chaser, so to speak. This combo, the cake and milk is Susan's one concession to an unhealthy diet. I on the other hand would have the cake topped with ice cream if she let me, and it would only be one of many concessions to a diet a nutritionist would be horrified at. After watching some more TV, Susan and I fall asleep with the set still on and blasting away (it's programmed to go off at one o'clock in the morning).

I usually drift off before Susan, but the last few nights have been different. I've had a lot of things to think about. That night she fell asleep before me and I lay awake. I had plans to be formulated so I left the warmth of our bed and walked the floor smoking one cigarette after another into the wee hours of the morning digesting all the information gleaned from cyber space and my bookshelf. Finally, just before dawn I had a plan, and satisfied there was nothing more to be learned or to be decided upon, fell into a deep untroubled dreamless sleep.

***

I awoke the next morning groggy and exhausted. A few hours of sleep is not enough for me so I took two Excedrin, and downed it with a cup of coffee to get the gears in motion. After a hearty breakfast of bacon and eggs (my choice) I told Susan not to bother me, and I entered my office, my private sanctuary, to prepare to put the plan into action.

I was going to try and open my soul to a parallel universe, a dimension of time and space called the "Quantum Vacuum", a dense cosmic medium that carries all the universal forces of nature where all events, and all experiences, past, present, and future are stored. This "new" science is nothing new to the Hindu religion. The Hindus have known about it for centuries although they call it by a different name, they call it the Akashic Records, or the Akashic Field. The field is a compendium of mystical knowledge encoded in a non-physical plane of existence. It contains all knowledge, and it can be accessed, and entered into through astral projection.

There are prerequisites to be able to have the paranormal work for you. Firstly you must believe there are forces at work outside our physical world. You have to accept that what we see, hear, touch, and feel are not the only realities. If you are a cynic, forget it. Non-believers have too many negative vibes to be able to break free and enter the next dimension. But since I have always believed in the mystical world what I had planned just might do the trick and cure me.

And so I began a warm up exercise, and the exercises would continue throughout the day. A treadmill, step machine or a set of weights is not required. It's not a regimen to develop a well sculptured body. It is a mental exercise to focus your mind to be in sync with your ethereal body, and it simply involves meditation. The protocol consists of segregating oneself in a serine environment free from all external noise or disturbances. And with eyes closed to avoid distractions Buddhist mantras are spoken over and over again. I don't think the chants have religious significance. It's just a meaningless monotonous sound that blocks out other thoughts and focuses your mind on the emptiness of space.

After awhile the physical body slows down, respiration drops, your muscles relax, and you gradually enter a semi trance state where time stands still. It's a peaceful and serene time totally void of unpleasant thoughts. You are oblivious of what is disturbing you, to what is going wrong in your life. You forget about the young hotshot trainee looking to replace you at your work place, or when you find out your kids have experimented with marijuana, or how are you going to pay next month's credit card and make the mortgage with the same paycheck. All the unpleasantness that clutters your mind is no longer a concern. It's like a misty fog that evaporates when the sky brightens and the sun comes out.

Buddhist and Hindu monks have been using meditation for over a thousand years as a means to liberate their inner self, their soul from their physical body so their ethereal being, their spirit, can be as one with the universe, and to find peace and contentment. I don't know what's out in the realm of endless time and space. It may only lead to an acceptance of ones fate, a resignation of things to come, and to be at peace with that knowledge. Or it may be a connection to a force field, a mysterious energy that has the power to heal, an energy that is often interpreted to be a miraculous cure.

I didn't think my conscious being, my rational mind would ever discover the secrets of the universe but my inner self might. Our inner self, our soul, at times referred to as our Astral Body or our Ethereal Body, is like a cumulus cloud floating across the sky. From afar we think we can grasp a cloud like a fluffy cotton ball, but when you reach for it, there is nothing there. It disappears into a vapor; something we know exists but cannot touch. It is as nebulous as a veiled dream, sometimes vivid for an instant, and then disjointed and fractured into a thousand pieces.

The Astral body is an entity from another dimension, and it exists within our human body. It is our inner self, our soul, and our true being within our physical shell. We mortals are only a vessel, something that can be discarded as a lobster sheds his shell, his exoskeleton. Consider an automobile.

We enter the vehicle and it takes us where we want to go. It has no mind, no soul, and when it wears out we discard it and get a new one. So it is with the Astral body, it is eternal. When our body dies the ethereal sprit leaves our physical remains and enters the Akashic dimension where it resides and blends with all the souls that ever lived, or ever will live and waits for an available human body to be born so that it may reincarnate and perpetuate the endless cycle of life and death, for all eternity.

These theories may be far out, but they offer a reasonable explanation as to how a psychic such as Edgar Cayce, perhaps the most famous clairvoyant of the twentieth century, was able to diagnose and cure many diseases. People seeking medical help would contact Cayce, and he while in a hypnotic trance would diagnose the illness and suggest a treatment to affect a cure. Cayce's secretary would document, and pass on to the patient his findings, even though the patient might be a thousand miles away.

It is believed that Cayce, while in a somnolent state, entered into the universal knowledge base of the Akashic field and drew from it the information he needed to affect the holistic cures for his patients. All knowledge that ever was, or will be: the past, the present, and the future reside in those records. The paranormal, from remote viewing, to telepathy, to faith healing, makes sense if you accept the concept of a universal repository, the Akashic dimension. It exists right here on earth parallel to our world but unseen by all but a few. It's a cosmic nebulous of immortal entities that at times can be contacted, and sometimes brought back to our dimension to work with us to help solve our earthly everyday problems, and unfortunately, at times to cause chaos.

Saturday morning

Saturday is the day when I usually become a couch potato, eat potato chips and drink beer all day while watching college football games from the comfort of an overstuffed armchair. However this was not just another Saturday for me, it is a day that would bring me closer to the end of days. No time for football, I had work to do. Today is the day I would put yesterday's meditation session to the test, to see if I could do what Edgar Cayce did, to enter the Akashic dimension and locate a soul who could cure me. One good thing: my doctor didn't work on Saturday. I didn't have to worry that he might call to see how I was feeling, and to tell me when the biopsy was scheduled. It was a concern of mine that Susan might pick up the phone when he called - before I had a chance to answer it, and I didn't want to ruin her weekend. She was still unaware of my condition, and I wanted to be the one to tell her, not the doctor.

After breakfast I locked myself in my office and set up the Ouija board, the portal to the spiritual world, the mystical device that might summon a spirit from beyond.

I considered quite a few unconventional options to supplement the traditional treatments the doctors would prescribe, and the Ouija board, the mystical oracle, seemed to offer the best odds in my life or death bet. However crazy as it might seem what I was about to attempt might eliminate the malignancy and cure me even though there was considerable danger involved, danger to myself, and danger to the world at large.

***

The Ouija board is a capricious device. At times it can be fanciful, funny and playful. I used to think it was a game; however I can assure you it certainly is not. Sometimes it is a dangerous entrance to places you may not want to go. To paraphrase Forest Gump, "It's like a box of chocolate; you never know what you might get."

Susan and I had used the board in the past. The first few sessions were fun. It was a good party game played with friends. A long time ago, when Susan and I were just starting out as a married couple, when neither we nor our friends had money to go dancing or to a movie, we spent Saturday nights at our house or one of our friend's home playing cards or board games. My favorite activity often had some involvement with the occult. We experimented with séances, holding hands around a dimly lit table trying to coax a reluctant ghost out of the spirit world. But a ghost in a physical form, one we could actually see, never visited us. However the Ouija board occasionally yielded positive results, and we didn't care if the answers to our questions were ambiguous with little validity. It was always fun.

We would gather around the kitchen table and set up the board prepared to have a pleasant evening regardless of what a ghostly spirit might or might not say. We asked Ouija many things. Will we have children? Will we be successful? Will we ever be able to afford a house in the suburbs? Usually a spirit willing to communicate with us would respond with a yes or no answer. Yes and no answers were easy for a spirit; spelling out words was not quite as easy. (Especially since we knew that we players had the choice of consciously moving the disk.) However once in a while we had interesting and often funny responses which none of us could have predicated. The spirit would be playful and humorous and at other times malicious and evil.

A funny incident took place shortly after Susan and I had returned to the states, after I completed my military tour in Germany. We were still considered newlyweds, and it was at a time when most of our friends were getting married. Sara and Bob were one of the couples who were tying the knot, and Susan and I had a date with them two weeks before their wedding date. Most of their nuptial plans had been completed: the chapel had been selected, the guest list compiled, invitations mailed, the reception, and the honeymoon reservations made. Everything was done except for having a place to live when they returned from their honeymoon. They had not yet found an apartment to rent as they were holding out for a unit in a building Bob's parents lived in. It was a beautiful rent controlled apartment in Flushing, and the rental agent assured Bob that there would be a vacancy in October.

The incident took place one Saturday night when Sara and Bob came to our home to play Canasta. But once we were seated around the card table Bob said,

"What do you say we skip the card games and check out the Ouija board? We still haven't found an apartment. Let's see what the spirits say about it." So they asked the Ouija what to do. The question went like this,

"Oh wise Ouija, shall we wait for the Flushing apartment to be available or should we not take a chance and rent an available apartment now before the wedding?" The spirit answered our question. It actually spelled out words, something very unusual because as I said earlier it generally only answers questions by having the planchette, the movable disk with a pointer, move to the "yes" or "no" portion of the board. This time it spelled out the words, "FLUSHING OCTOBER."

Our friends were ecstatic. Their problem solved. They married and went on their honeymoon without a care in the world. When they returned in October they found the apartment was not available after all, and they had to rent elsewhere.

A few years later we happened to be playing bridge with Sara and Bob in their apartment, the rent controlled one in Flushing, the one they sought when they first got married. We began reminiscing about old times, and at one point I said, "Bob, remember when you got married and put so much stock in the Ouija board that you never rented an apartment before you got married?"

"You bet, I remember it well. We wound up in a crummy little apartment in Bayside until we got this place." We laughed over that, and then I asked,

"By the way when did you get this apartment?" He considered the question, his eyes widened, and then realization dawned on him,

"It was in October, just like Ouija had predicated, but two years after our wedding."

Unfortunately the last time we played with the oracle we experienced disturbing results, and Susan insisted we never use it again. She made me promise to throw it out, but I never did. Instead I hid it in the garage with all the other junk that was squirreled away. It's my nature to never throw out anything.

The incident that prompted Susan to get rid of the Ouija board was several years after the Sara and Bob incident. We had relocated to the suburbs and the Ouija board got buried and forgotten in the move. We had other interests. Work, children, our new lifestyle, all of these things became more important, and the supernatural world which fascinated us in the past was forgotten. But one Saturday night when some friends were at our house for small talk, coffee, and cake, the conversation turned to the paranormal. I said,

"Hey, I have an Ouija board in the garage. Let's give it a shot and see what it says." Susan didn't like the idea, but I prevailed. I found the board in the garage and set it up.

We usually start the session by asking the question: "Oh wise Ouija, do you have any message for us tonight?"

To our amazement the planchette began to whorl about at an almost uncontrollable speed. Suddenly it stopped. And it stopped so abruptly that our fingers slid off the disk. We placed our fingers back on the planchette and once again it began to move, but more slowly this time. It finally halted at a letter in the alphabet for a few seconds and then resumed its travel, but each time it stopped, it pointed to a letter. We recorded the letters and when the disk would move no more we realized that it spelled out the word "PAUL". One of our friends sitting at the table was named Paul, and we looked at him in wonderment. What could this mean? What message did the spirits have for him?

That evening my son was also entertaining a friend. The boys were in the basement playroom doing their thing, and as we discussed the meaning of the cryptic message my son ran up the stairs with his friend who also happened to be named Paul. The young Paul was white as a ghost. His eyes were two ping-pong balls popping out of his eye sockets. I never saw anything like it. I actually thought his eyes might detach from his head and bounce across the floor.

The boy was a neighbor who lived next door, and Susan upon seeing his condition, scooped him up and carried him home. His mother was horrified when she saw her son, but was calm enough to drive the boy to the hospital a few blocks away.

The incident sobered us, and we moved into the kitchen for coffee and cake. Usually desert was a pleasant time, a prelude to ending the evening. It was a time we could joke about the mistakes we made in the bridge game, or discuss the latest gossip. But that night we were sober and pensive anxiously awaiting news about Paul. When Paul's mother returned from the emergency room she told us his eyes had returned to normal as they entered the hospital, and after an examination, the doctor could find nothing wrong. Needless to say, that was the end of our experimentation with the board for good. Susan never wanted to see it again, and she asked me to dispose of it immediately. But I didn't. It went into our garage, out of sight, with all my other junk.

***

An Ouija board is a portal to the other side. The other side of what I don't know. It may be to another dimension, one that co-exists with our world but invisible to the eye and undetectable to scientific instruments. It may be a door to heaven where fortunate spirits abide or it might be a door to hell where demons and monsters lurk waiting for the opportunity to come back into our world for their own nefarious reasons. Perhaps it is an opening to purgatory, a home for lost souls awaiting their final destiny. I personally think the Ouija is a tool that allows one to enter into the Akashic field, where the disembodied ethereal spirits reside, and I believe if I can synchronize my mind's energy with the field, I will be able to tap into its resources, and draw from that mysterious place, the means to make my body whole again.

At any rate, this is my plan, and it's the only one I have. I intend to once again access the spirit world through the Ouija. It's a dangerous game I'm about to play. I'm going to be sliding down a slippery slope, and I hope it works. There is no guarantee that it would connect me with a good spirit. It might turn out to be a Pandora's box capable of unleashing untold horrors into my physical body.

Remember the movie, *The Exorcist*? It was based on a real incident. It involved a thirteen-year-old youth named Robbie, a boy who lived in Maryland. Robbie was fascinated with, and enjoyed partnering with his maternal grandmother to ask Ouija questions relating to everyday matters, and his future prospects. Eventually his grandmother passed away but Robbie continued seeking advice from the oracle on his own, without a partner. During one session, on or about January 15th, 1949, a demon or evil spirit entered the boys' body via the Ouija board and took possession of his soul. It took months of continual prayer for a team of Catholic priests headed by a priest named Father Hughes to exorcise the demon.

Saturday night

Susan and I are staying home. We haven't any plans for the evening. Usually we spend a Saturday night with friends, not that we have many anymore. A few of them moved out of state to be closer to their grandchildren. Others have retired to Florida, and a few more have passed away. There was nothing I wanted to see at the movies or at our local playhouse theatre, and we only go to restaurants during the week when the service and food is better, so I guess it's another night at home. I suppose we are getting old; inertia is setting in. It's easier to do nothing at all than to actually get out of the house to have some fun. Besides we and our friends are grandparents now, and Saturday night socializing is less frequent as our children want to go out on the weekend, and we grandparents get stuck babysitting. History repeats itself. Forty years ago, when Susan and I had young children, we expected our parents to baby-sit for us so we could have a night out. What goes around comes around.

Normally if Susan and I did not have plans for a Saturday night she would rent a movie at Blockbusters, and we would relax at home with a bag of popcorn while watching a DVD. But I begged off the movie as I was anxious to begin the cure. Susan raised her eyebrows and gave me a funny look when I told her I had other things to do. She is beginning to get suspicious. I always want to watch a movie when there was nothing else to do. She knows something is up. I'm usually the one who looked forward to getting into bed with a bag of popcorn or an overstuffed sandwich, and watch a good flick. But when I told her I wanted to finish up some things in the office Susan smiled and said sarcastically,

"If I catch you with some online girlfriend you are going to pay dearly."

I hoped she meant a new diamond ring, and not divorce. A ring is a lot less expensive.

After dinner I entered my office, closed the door, and turned off the computer. This was a departure from the norm as I almost always access the computer when entering the office, and I'm positive the silence alerted Susan to something being wrong. For sure she would have to know the truth soon.

The Ouija board was hidden in plain sight, under a stack of papers, and I retrieved it and set it upon the desk top. Hiding things on my desk is the best place to hide anything. Susan doesn't touch papers on my desk. She has enough of her own work to do without looking at mine.

I set up the board but left the planchette in the game box. I didn't want the distraction of a moving disc interrupting my thoughts, nor should I say my lack of conscious thoughts, because I was not going to ask Ouija a question. My intention was to open up a portal to the other side to let an entity pass through to our world. I would place my fingertips on the board and meditate, to open my mind and body to whomever or whatever wanted to enter. My subconscious mind knew what was needed without any conscious interference. And if there happened to be a roaming, restless entity visiting our world, and he wanted to enter my body to affect a cure, he was free to do so through the Ouija board.

After a last smoke to calm my nerves I sat in the office chair, reclined it to the maximum horizontal position, kicked off my shoes, closed my eyes, and silently began a Buddhist mantra. Over and over I repeated the chant, and all the while visualizing, and watching through my mind's eye vapors entering and exiting my nostrils. The slower I inhaled and exhaled the clearer and more distinct the vapors appeared. It looked like the smoke from a burning candle drifting upward in a draft free environment. It was beautiful to watch, and I could feel my body relaxing, my heartbeat becoming slower, my limbs going limp. I was entering into a hypnotic trance.

Visualizing a meaningless moving object focuses your mind on something without actually thinking about anything. It induces a mesmerized state of mind. I suppose watching sheep jump over fences might work just as well but the smoke works for me and I often use it to fall asleep when the tensions of daily life would otherwise have kept me awake.

The mental visualization of the vapors coupled with the Buddhist meditation placed me in the deepest trance I have ever been in. I don't know how much time passed or how long I was in a hypnotized state but suddenly I awoke with a start and a searing pain in my chest. It was a pain unlike any I had ever experienced. It felt as though my lungs were being torn out. *Oh shit, what the hell has happened to me? Did I give myself a heart attack?* I was scared, more scared than I have ever been, and I rested for a while until my heart stopped racing and the pain subsided. That was it for the night. I left the room shaken and trembling, and joined Susan. She was in bed reading a book. She looked up at me and said in an exaggerated icy but friendly tone,

"Oh, did your online girl friend leave you for someone else?"

I answered with a smile on my face,

"Yes. My prepaid debit card ran out of funds."

That night I once again tossed and turned in the bed unable to sleep. I paced the floors smoking one cigarette after another. After a while I went outside into the cold November night and looked up into the sky. It must have been the phase of a new moon because the night was so dark you could hardly see your hand in front of your face. But when I looked up the sky was peppered with stars from horizon to horizon. I hadn't seen a sight like that since we camped out in the woods with the kids when they were still young children, when we were in a forest so thick and remote that the city lights did not dispel the darkness of the night. I was filled with awe and wonderment and thought, *how vast the sky, how insignificant we are, just grains of sand on an endless beach.*

Monday

I took a time out yesterday, and I think I'll do the same today. I'm getting too anxious over finding a cure. The pain I felt in my chest while under the trance the previous night scared the crap out of me. Now I don't know what to do. If I attempt another hypnotic session it might kill me. Dead from a heart attack is far worse than a disease that may never put me in the grave. I think I'll wait until the doctor tells me how serious this cancer is before attempting any more self-cures.

Tuesday

Late yesterday afternoon, Dr. Rubins, our family doctor, the physician who made the initial diagnosis phoned me. He said he had secured a time slot at the hospital for a biopsy on Thursday. This meant I would have to go to the hospital on Wednesday for the pre-op work. I didn't need another physical before the biopsy as I had one a week earlier at the doctor's office during my annual physical exam. That was the day when the x-ray portion of the exam indicated a spot on my lung as a possible malignant tumor.

Doctor Rubins has a modern Hi-Tech office and he buys every new toy on the market. One of them was a new x-ray machine and he uses it whenever possible. Of course he doesn't care what the hi-tech toys cost as they are profit centers. His patients pay dearly for the machines either directly or through the insurance company with a little profit left over to cover the payments for his thirty-five foot sailboat and Mercedes roadster. And so his assistant took the pictures, developed them, and brought the film to the doctor during the consult session that took place after the blood work and other routine tests were completed. The consultation was the final part of the physical, it's when he sits me down in his office and tells me to lose weight, quit smoking and watch my diet. I have always ignored his warnings in the past but thank God reviewing the x-ray was also part of the consultation.

The surgeon clipped the film on to the wall-viewing screen and studied it for a few minutes. He had a concerned look on his face, and said,

"I see what may be a spot on your lung but let's not jump to conclusions. X-rays are inconclusive. I'll schedule a CAT scan; it will give us a more accurate picture of the situation."

I think I turned white and almost passed out at the news because he asked me if I was all right. I said "yes", but I thought "no".

I went to the radiology center two days later, spent what seemed like an hour in the "tunnel of fear", and received the bad news via the telephone from Dr. Rubins the following day. The results confirmed the original x-rays that were taken during the physical. The scan indicated a lung malignancy although only a biopsy could tell for sure. Later that night while lying in bed is when I played the pinball machine on the ceiling, and paced the floors until the wee hours of the morning.

***

A week has passed since receiving the results of the CT scan, and as much as I hated to, I have to break the bad news to Susan. I intend to drive myself to the pre-op screening but she would have to drive me to the hospital on the day of the biopsy so she would have to know the truth. The information couldn't be kept from her any longer.

When I finally told Susan the results of the scan she cried. I expected that. Most women cry when things get out of their control. It doesn't matter how old a woman is, or how calloused she may become after dealing with all they have to manage: work, the household, the children and their problems, and in Susan's case, me. Women shed tears, sometimes for a good reason, and sometimes for no reason at all. Maybe that's why they live longer than men. They get it out of their system all in one shot, and don't let it fester. Maybe we can learn something from the fair sex.

Wednesday

I drove myself to the hospital this morning for the pre-op work and checked in at the admissions desk. I'm sure the forms you must fill out are just a subterfuge for what they really want, your insurance card. After proving I could pay for the procedure the clerk presented me with a few forms to fill out, the most important one (for the hospital, and for the surgeon) being the document that made me swear not to sue them if something went wrong. I updated my living will and signed organ donor forms, and wondered if cancer laced cells are acceptable? If they want this worn out body they could have it, and good luck to the recipient. The nurse drew a little blood, the lab technician took another x-ray, and I signed another release, and went home.

Susan was anxiously awaiting my arrival. When I was settled in she made a pot of coffee and some freshly baked snacks, and we sat at the kitchen table discussing the admission procedures while I drank a steaming hot cup of Jamaica Green Mountain brew, and munched on my favorite snack food, freshly baked brownies. I told her all the things that had transpired. Actually she gave me the third degree. Susan knows nothing about hospital procedures. She hasn't been to a hospital, except for visiting friends in over forty years. Nor does she take any medication or have annual physicals. She is one of the healthiest physical wrecks you have ever encountered. She has a constant cough from smoking, bad knees, and silently endures the arthritic aches and pains that wrack her body. But Susan still manages to play tennis twice a week, cook, clean, run the office and do anything a thirty year old can do, only better. She is amazing.

***

Talking about the admissions procedure brought to mind a very unusual incident that took place. While I was in the admissions office filling out the required forms I dropped my pen on the floor and picked it up with my left hand. And then, not thinking, signed the form with the same hand. But now that I recall the incident I wonder how I did that. I'm right handed.

***

That night I reviewed the day's events in my mind while in bed staring into space. Everything was going well. Susan stopped crying and has accepted the fact that she might be alone sooner than expected. She is hopeless optimist and that's one of the things I love about her. She is a modern Candide in this best of all worlds. Or perhaps she is an ostrich with her head in the sand. Whatever, she always sees the bright side of things and accepts life as it is handed out, be it good or bad. On the other hand I always prepare for the worst. I'm not a pessimist by any definition of the word. I'm just ready for any contingency, and while I sometimes have moments of depression, they never last very long. And given the situation I currently face I should be depressed. It would be understandable, and justified. I should not only be concerned, but also be worried. I was worried about my future a few days ago, after the initial x-ray. But now it's like a curtain has been lifted. For some reason I consider the impending biopsy an inconvenience, something that is going to interfere with my morning tennis game. Oh well it's something I have to do to keep Susan from bugging me. With that thought in mind I rolled over on my side and went to sleep. But before I dozed off I realized that I didn't have my last cigarette, and I always have a last cigarette before going to bed. This time I didn't even think about it.

Thursday

Today is the big day, the day I would go under the biopsy knife, and I had to get up early to be at the hospital by 6:30 AM as I was scheduled for the first surgery of the day. Normally I sleep until the sunlight shinning through the ill fitting vertical blinds gets me up. But I was happy to awake early and get the procedure over with as I was not allowed to eat anything after dinner the night before, and I was hungry. Susan and I usually consume a thick slice of chocolate cake washed down with a glass of milk before going to sleep, and I missed not having the late night snack. Think that's the reason we are both twenty pounds overweight?

After checking into the hospital a burley orderly strapped me into a wheelchair and brought me to the O.R. Did they think I was a cripple? Did they think I might get up and bolt? Well, I'm sure some people do bug out and I guess they didn't want to take the chance that I would get up and run for the door. After undressing and getting into an immodest robe that was missing the tie strings, and being placed on a gurney, I was prepped for the biopsy. I thought the whole thing was a bit of overkill. *For God's sake, it's only a biopsy. What do they do for the actual surgery?*

The nurse inserted an I.V. in my left arm, drew some blood from the right arm and then pushed the gurney into a corner to await the surgeon's arrival. I waited for what seemed a long time although it probably was no more than half an hour. I was beginning to feel the anger start to fester. *Where the hell is the doctor? I showed up on time for the surgery, the bastard could show some consideration and be on time; he gets paid enough.*

Finally the surgeon arrived. He had the latest x-rays in his hand and a perplexed look on his face. That didn't look good.

The surgeon came over and introduced himself in a barely understandable Indian accent and said,

"Hi, I'm Doctor Singh. Doctor Phillips is out with the flu, and I'll be doing the biopsy today. But first there are some things I want to talk about. I have the x-rays that were taken earlier, but I never had the chance to examine the originals, or the scan. I only saw the print out."

He hesitated for a moment, looked pensive and said, "Hang in there; I'll be right back. I want to look at the original x-rays before starting the procedure."

And with that statement he quickly turned on his heels and left the room. Not a word of comfort, or an explanation. Wild angry thoughts raced through my head, *Jesus Christ, he must have been absent when they taught bedside manner at his Mickey-mouse medical school, or do they even teach patient care in India. If I required surgery I would insist on an American surgeon, this guy might not even have a green card. Can Susan sue if an Indian doctor screwed up and I didn't make it?* I was more angry than concerned, but I did wonder what could be wrong. *Am I too far gone for the doctor to even perform a biopsy?*

I lay strapped in the gurney facing the clock on the wall, and watched the hand advance minute by minute. I started to sweat even though the room was kept at an extremely low temperature. What the hell was going on?

Doctor Singh finally returned, x-rays in his hand. He still looked perplexed.

"I looked at the original x-rays, and clearly there seems to be a tumor on your lung, but the latest x-rays only show a dark gray area, and I don't think it's a tumor.

"Well I'm here now. Can't you go in and see if it really is a cancer? Is it a big deal? I sure don't want to go through this again if I don't have to."

"Yes, we might as well get it over with."

What he didn't say, but I'm sure he was thinking was, "I'm not going to waste a morning and not get paid".

The surgeon left the prep room, and I waited a while longer until the anesthesiologist appeared. He seemed like a nice guy, an American for a change. "You OK?" he asked as he proceeded to inject the anesthesia into the I.V. He didn't even wait for my answer, the asshole. Suppose I wasn't okay? I was then wheeled into the O.R. and it's the last thing I remember until I woke up in the recovery room a short time later. My throat hurt, and I coughed up a little blood, but otherwise I was intact. After a while Dr. Singh returned and said,

"I went down your throat and snipped some lung tissue. It's being sent off to the lab, and I should have the results in a day or two. If you have any problems Dr. Rubins will take care of it or he will call me."

With that statement he turned and left the room. My final thought before dozing off again was that he must get paid for cutting, but not for communicating.

When I awoke I felt fine except my throat still hurt. They wheeled the rolling gurney down to the outpatient ward, transferred me to a bed, gave me some juice, and offered coffee. I passed on the coffee. I've had hospital coffee before. No thanks. A few hours later Susan came and took me home. It was 1:00 PM. I guess Medicare doesn't pay for extended hospital stays.

***

Once home Susan made buttered toast and a pot of hot tea. That, and a bowl of chicken soup, is the Jewish equivalent of penicillin. I drank the tea and skipped the toast. My throat still hurt; I just wanted to get into bed. But Susan had other plans. She had to know every detail of the procedure. She asked question after question, and I had no answers.

"How did it go?" she asked

"Okay, I guess"

"Do you have cancer?"

"I don't know. It was only a biopsy."

"When will you find out?"

"I don't know that either, all I know is that I want to get into bed."

I was starting to get annoyed. She was becoming a pest, a pain in the ass. I lashed out at her.

"For God's sake, will you please shut the fuck up and leave me alone", I yelled back at her.

Susan stopped dead in her tracks, mouth wide open, and just stared at me. I have never shouted at her like that before and never used curse words. *Why am I so angry all the time? What the hell is wrong with me?*

Monday

I heard from Dr. Rubins today. The results were in. The biopsy was negative, no sign of a malignancy. Susan was happy. She was overjoyed, and I should have been happy too, but I was just annoyed they put me through so much trouble for nothing. What a waste of time.

Later, over coffee with Susan, I noticed she was very quiet and pensive. She is usually bubbly and gregarious, chatting away like a magpie. But today she was subdued as if there was something on her mind she didn't want to talk about.

"What the hell is wrong now?" I said.

"There's nothing wrong with me but there's something wrong with you. What are you so angry about? Nothing I do makes you happy anymore. Why are you so mad all the time?"

"Dogs get mad, people get angry. Can't you even speak the Kings English anymore, dummy?"

With that statement Susan bolted away from the table, and ran upstairs, tears flowing. I stayed and finished my coffee. *Piss on her, she's too God damned sensitive, and I'm tired of catering to her fucking moods.*

That night as I lay in bed staring at the ceiling I thought about all that had transpired over the past few weeks. When everyone assumed that I had cancer I thought it was the end. And when I had an almost unbearable searing pain in my chest while under self-hypnosis I thought I would certainly die of a heart attack. And now I am cancer free, and healthy, and never felt better. Life certainly is a mystery.

"Wait a minute", I thought, "The Ouija session must have worked. The first x-ray and the MRI confirmed a tumor yet there was none when they performed the biopsy. The Ouija must have initiated a miraculous cure. No - The Ouija can't cure anything. It is only a window to the other side. As I went into a trance I concentrated on a spirit from inside the Akashic dimension reaching out and curing me. But that couldn't be right either. Ethereal entities can't affect a cure from outside your body. They must leave the Akashic world and enter your physical shell, do their work and hopefully leave. Only I didn't think it ever left.

My situation mirrors the movie, *The Exorcist*, or the real life experience of the boy from Maryland in the 1940's. It wasn't an evil spirit who entered my body; it was just a healthy bad tempered entity looking for a new home. *Does this mean I have two spirits living inside me? Am I some sort of Doctor Jekyll and Mister Hyde?*

Tuesday

Monday night I had an epiphany while lying in bed waiting for sleep to envelop me, and I had been giving it some thought today. I've changed, that's for sure. Aside from being left handed, off cigarettes, and short tempered, I am a totally different person. The short fuse and anger may only be a temporary condition probably brought on by the anxiety of the cancer scare. At least I hope so. On the positive side of things, I seem to think more clearly now. I feel more confident. I'm not so much of a patsy. I used to kowtow to Susan all the time just to keep her happy. Well it's time for someone to make me happy. I've also lost some of my unfounded prejudices. I don't think that hunters or hunting is so bad. It's just a matter of personal freedom. And the government should keep its nose out of our business. I can't believe I used to call myself liberal. God damned liberals should go to hell.

Thursday

I've stopped recording each and every day. Oh, I'll keep a diary, but only when there is something important to relate, a chronicle of events so to speak. It's important to keep track of the meaningful days and how my mood swings cycle from good to bad, from high to low. It's more than something I want to do – it's something I must do. I may be on to something big with the Ouija board phenomenon, and it must be memorialized and documented. Who knows, right now I am doctor Frankenstein and his creation all rolled up into one big monster. But maybe everything will settle out for the good, and perhaps one day all of us, all humanity may be able to contact the Akashic dimension as easily as picking up the telephone. Perhaps my personal experiences may contribute in some small way to the repository of esoteric knowledge, and my angry, tormented life may be of some value to mankind.

Friday

One day runs into the next. I'm retired so there is nothing pressing. But I am getting restless. Susan said I should do volunteer work at the hospital. I thought it was a dumb idea. With the money they charge they should be able to pay people to do the work. And volunteers get all the crappy jobs, like pushing a cart full of books to the patients' rooms. A trained monkey could do that. She also suggested I volunteer at a soup kitchen for the homeless and unemployed. That galled me even more. There are plenty of jobs out there, maybe not jobs paying in six figures, but a lot of these homeless bums could work at McDonalds, or be a bus boy in a restaurant. That's the trouble with this country; nobody wants to work. In the depression days, in the 1930's, there wasn't any government unemployment checks but people survived. Today everyone expects someone else to take care of him or her. Everyone expects handouts. No one gave me a handout when I was growing up.

***

Susan is getting to be a real pain in the ass. She is still working in our office and she expects me to help with the housework. Well that's not happening, at least not on a regular basis. I didn't sign on to be a houseboy or a maid. But if I didn't empty the dishwasher or vacuum the floors once in a while the house would be a pigpen. And she is not going to spend our money for outside help either if I have a say in the matter. My mom raised us kids just fine. She had a job and my dad never had to work around the house. I think women today have it too easy. For Christ sake, they hardly cook anymore. They don't even have to peel a potato. Just open a bag of frozen spuds and veggies. And that's the way it is with all food. Everything is quick frozen or a prepared meal. Women today don't know what a hard day's work is. They are setting a bad example for the next generation. That's why kids are so lazy. All they think about is getting high and texting one another. They should follow the Chinese example. Now those Chinks know how to work, and they don't live on government handouts either.

Talking about woman not cooking real meals anymore reminds me of an incident that took place the other day. Susan and I went to the supermarket and we had a hell of a fight right in the store. I'm only mentioning this because going shopping with her is another thing I seldom have done in the past. I have always hated grocery shopping. I've always thought that it's a waste of time for both of us to do something that she could do without me. But that day I decided we were spending too much of our budget on food, and I was going to make some suggestions on how to save some money.

We were at the meat department and as usual Susan was picking out prime cuts of meat, things like center cut lamb chops, not the shoulder cuts, and the most expensive steaks. I interceded and suggested she buy something less expensive.

"Honey, you have a slow cooker sitting on a shelf in the pantry, the one the kids got us for Christmas a few years ago, and you never have used it, not even once", I said in my most pleasant voice, "Why not get some less expensive food like the stewing beef and cook them in the slow cooker?"

"You got to be kidding. It will take all day to cook and it will still taste like shoe leather"

"That's bull shit. It's not going to be tough, not if you take the time to cook it properly"

"Well, okay, maybe it won't be tough but it will be tasteless"

My composure was beginning to wear thin and I started to raise my voice.

"God damn it if you spent some more time in the kitchen maybe you could figure out how to fix a proper meal. A five year old could do what you do, open a bag of frozen crap, toss it in the microwave and burn a steak."

Well you get the idea, the argument escalated and it was mostly one sided, my side. I lost control and started yelling obscenities at Susan, and many of the shoppers took notice. I should have been embarrassed, but I was not. They can all go to hell.

***

I don't think I can take it anymore. Life with Susan is getting unbearable. Everything she does drives me crazy, and gets on my nerves. She works during the day and we don't interact much so there are few arguments. In the evening conversation is also at a minimum as we watch TV in the bedroom, and we usually tune in the shows Susan chooses. Occasionally when there is really nothing on but trash that even she won't watch she lets me see what I'm interested in. But then Susan makes comments like, "Enough already with the military channel, how many times can you watch the Battle for Stalingrad?

I usually just keep my mouth shut, watch the show, and brood in silence. After a few hours of mind numbing television the TV timer kicks in and Susan is out like a light, and I lay awake for hours. Who can sleep when she snores like a sick cow?

***

I slept in the guest room last night. Susan and I had a fight while in bed watching TV. I don't even remember what it was about, just a lot of little things which normally doesn't amount to a pile of beans. Oh, I remember what sent me into the guest room; it was concerning my son Bruce. I said I didn't think he was carrying his weight. Susan being a typical mother defended him. She argued that Bruce has a daughter now and was justified in wanting to spend some time with her. I think, and have always thought the business comes first, and a person must do what he has to do. If it requires working ten hours a day, seven days a week for a few months, well that's the way it goes. I've had disagreements with Susan before over this subject, and I usually see her point and ease up on the kid. But this time we had a full-blown argument, and my tone was more venomous than usual. The argument brought on the tears, and I grabbed a pillow off the bed and headed for the spare bedroom.

***

This morning, after waking up early, I fixed a single cup of coffee for myself. I usually get up before Susan, fix a pot of coffee, and drink a cup while scanning the news on my computer. Then I wake her and we have breakfast together. But today I was still angry over last night's argument so I let her sleep. I dressed, grabbed my laptop, left the house, and drove to the village center, to the local McDonalds.

Sometimes I'll have a burger at a Wendy's or a McDonalds, but never a breakfast. I tried a breakfast once a long time ago when Susan and I were on vacation, and we were very disappointed. I swore I'd starve to death before eating anything other than a burger at a franchised restaurant, and I don't know what prompted me to do so this morning. As I recall when we breakfasted at a fast food restaurant the scrambled eggs were hard and dry as a piece of beef jerky. I've had dehydrated and reconstituted eggs while in the Air Force that tasted better. Susan had pancakes that looked more like cardboard than real food, and served with something that is supposed to pass for syrup. We both said, "Never again".

As I said, I don't know why I chose McDonalds for breakfast since I only have bad memories of pre-prepared food, but I ordered a breakfast sandwich, an egg McMuffin and actually enjoyed it. I also liked the solitude, being alone for a change, and not having to deal with a waitress. Just let me eat my meal and leave me alone.

The restaurant had a Wi-Fi hotspot so I relaxed with the coffee and savored the quiet time while checking the e-mail on my laptop. Usually there are twenty-five pieces of junk mail that I instantly delete and a joke or two from friends who think keeping in touch is by forwarding jokes they receive to everyone in their address book. But today there was one e-mail I looked forward to receiving. It was from the gun shop. My shotgun was ready to be picked up.

***

Normally I never go out of town in the morning due to the rush hour traffic on the thruway, but I couldn't wait to get my hands on the gun. This was another new side of my personality. I never condoned hunting nor did I ever own a weapon, and if it weren't for the possibility I might have to use the gun on myself I never would have bought one.

While driving to Jackson, to the sporting goods shop, my thoughts drifted to the initial visit to the store. A week earlier the idea of owning a gun was something I would never have thought of. I have never hunted or killed anything, not even a mouse that once shared our home, and I thought men who hunted were no better than predatory animals.

On the first trip to the gun shop I thought the little toad that waited on me should face a grizzly bear with a malfunctioning rifle. I imagined a scenario whereby he would be in the woods, see a bear, raise the gun to his shoulder, take aim, squeeze the trigger, and only hear a click as the firing pin contacted an empty chamber. Then the bear would charge him, claws extended, and fangs bared to rend his flesh into little scraps of meat. But this time I actually looked forward to meeting with the salesman. He was a hunter, but so what. Lots of people are hunters. No big deal.

When I entered the gun shop the little salesman recognized me immediately and greeted me warmly. He retrieved the gun from the stock room and I paid for the weapon with cash so Susan would not know about the purchase. She paid the credit card bills and I had to keep her out of the loop lest she hassle me over owning a weapon. The salesman included a box of ammunitions gratis and instructed me on the gun's use, its safety features, cleaning instructions, and so forth. This guy certainly loved to talk, and I found him interesting. He wasn't such a bad guy after all. We got along so well that I set a date with him to go target shooting and perhaps a hunting trip.

As I exited the store and entered the parking area I noticed a young man walking out of the lot. This struck me as quite unusual as the neighborhood is predominantly African-American and this guy was white. Normally the only Caucasians you see are not pedestrians but people in cars just speeding through the town hoping their automobile would not break down within the city environs. The guy definitely didn't belong in this neighborhood, and his furtive glances made him look even more suspicious. He appeared to be in his late twenties, thin and scruffy looking. His face was severely pockmarked and it was evident he hadn't shaved in at least a week. He was wearing worn out grimy jeans, a dirty hoodie sweatshirt, and he carried a knapsack slung over his shoulder. I wondered why he was even in the lot. He was not a shopper and the parking area was an enclosed fenced in space. Obviously he could not be using it for a short cut to another street.

There were only three cars in the lot, the two salesmen's and mine, and the dude appeared to be headed away from my BMW. I quickly walked over to my car and noticed a small scratch on the door just above the lock and below the window. The lock had been jimmied. The hooded guy must have broken into the car while I was shopping.

I opened the unlocked door and immediately saw the GPS cradle was empty, the navigation unit missing, and the laptop I had left on the passengers' seat was gone. I was furious and got into the car, started it up and exited the lot looking for the alleged thief. I spotted him almost immediately. He was down the block and turning into a side street. I followed, stopped short of my destination for a minute to remove the shotgun from the carry case, loaded it with a full clip of cartridges, chambered a round, and continued following him. He turned into a street leading to the next parallel avenue.

The entire area was deserted except for the man I was pursuing, no cars and no pedestrians. The few buildings facing the street were vacant and several windows on the first floor broken. The facades of the brick buildings were spray painted with graffiti identifying and staking out the turf of local gangs. The buildings were long past having any commercial value and more than likely scheduled for demolition to prevent drug users from setting up crack houses.

I pulled up to the curb and exited the car twenty feet behind the thief; it was time to act. This was one robbery that was going down bad for the robber for a change. I got out of my car and approached him. The shotgun was in my hand, the safety off, and I pointed it at the bandit.

"Okay asshole; let's see what you have in your knapsack."

He replied with a look of arrogance and contempt.

"Fuck you, old man,"

Immediately after cursing me he swung his knapsack at my head. Fortunately he missed his target but connected with my shoulder knocking me to the ground. My head bounced off the concrete sidewalk leaving me stunned and disoriented. The shotgun flew out of my hand and landed a few feet away leaving me defenseless. The thief looked down at my prostrate body and grinned, confidant that he now had the upper hand. I'm sure he thought this was going to be a bonus day. He had an easy mark that would add a shotgun and my wallet to his booty.

He slowly walked the few feet separating us and stood over me savoring the moment while reaching into his pocket and removing a switchblade knife. I must have looked so helpless that he didn't even bother to render me unconscious with a kick to my face or body. I suppose he thought I would stand up and submit to the mugging without his having to bend over and drag me to my feet. But he was wrong.

Feigning helplessness I sat up with outstretched pleading arms looking the part of a helpless victim. But I had a plan and I was not as defenseless as it appeared. I made an attempt to get up but purposely fell back to the ground. Meanwhile the thief just stood over me enjoying the moment.

"Get up old man and let's see what's in your wallet."

I made another attempt to get up but intentionally fell backwards and diagonally to the side placing me within reach of the shotgun. By now my head was clear and I knew the plan would work. I spun to the right and rolled over to the gun, picked it up with one motion, pointed the muzzle towards his chest and squeezed the trigger. The noise was deafening, and I was thrown back to the ground by the recoil of the weapon. I quickly scrambled back on my feet to see the damage that was wrought, to see if the thief was still a threat, to see if he was wounded or dead.

The blast sent the man flying into the building behind him. He hit the brick wall hard and slumped to the ground, his back propped up against the building, feet splayed out towards me. I smiled and thought he looked just like the rag doll I gave to my granddaughter last Christmas, minus the blood, of course. I didn't have to take his pulse to know he was dead. The bloody gore dripping down the brick wall more than likely was his heart. I retrieved the knapsack and inspected its contents. Sure enough, there was my laptop and GPS. There were also a few other personal possessions, one of which was a bag of white powder. It might have been sugar but I don't think so. I have never seen heroin before but I thought this must be the real thing. I reclaimed my belongings, kept his wallet, and dumped the dope into the street. The white powder dusting the black asphalt was just the right touch to make the incident seem to be a drug related murder and not high on the police priority list of must solve cases. After a quick scan of the area to make sure there were no witnesses I returned to my car and drove off thinking that I had just committed the perfect crime.

***

As I headed back home my heartbeat slowly returned to normal and I reviewed the incident over and over in my mind. There were no police cars burning rubber and following me in a high-speed chase. There were no outraged witnesses to the incident. And even if there were, witnesses to killings in crime-ridden neighborhoods such as this rarely come forward. The locals have a code of silence being fearful of retaliation by gang members. I had nothing to worry about except for the fact that I had just killed someone and how it might affect me. Would I have remorse and guilt to the extent that I might confess the crime to the police? Could I live with myself knowing I took a life in cold blood?

Suddenly it dawned on me. I realized I was thinking about the killing in a purely analytical way. It was not bothering me in the least; I had no remorse or regret. Aside from a rush of adrenalin and a rapid heartbeat I had less emotional feelings over the incident than I might have had while watching an exciting movie. I always thought if I ever got mugged I would be scared out of my mind and meekly submit to whatever demands the thief might make. But I was not frightened, my knees did not buckle, I did not faint. I was hardly fazed, and acted on reflex and never considering alternative measures to save my life or my possessions. I was as calm as a clam in the bottom of an ocean, like this killing might be a conditioned reflex, acquired through countless violent situations, something I had done so often that it was an automatic response.

I could never have been this unemotional and callous a month ago, and wouldn't even kill a spider that lived in our house. I would gently pick up and deposit the little creature into the backyard garden. I couldn't hurt anyone a month ago. It was not me who killed the unfortunate thief; it was my new entity.

I wondered who my new sprit might have been in his past life to be able to kill without remorse. Was he at one time or another a Mafia hit man, or perhaps a professional mercenary soldier who fought in the African Congo over a half century ago? I knew he was left-handed, didn't smoke, and was one angry short-tempered son of a bitch. But what else was there to know about him?

***

When I left the town of Jackson I headed towards the expressway, the fastest way to get back to my quiet village where nothing exciting ever happens, and the villagers are content to sit on their deck drinking a Bloody Mary instead of spilling blood. But I quickly realized that I had to make two stops before returning home. The first stop was to the local Walmart to buy a new jacket, and I drove there using side streets as that was the fastest route. Avoiding the highway and not having to keep alert for the maniac lane changers on the road also gave me more time to think. I had to plan an alibi in the unlikely event I might need one, and I needed to find an undetectable way to get rid of any evidence linking me to the crime.

One usually does not go on a shopping spree after committing a murder but there was backsplash blood on my jacket so it had to be replaced. I've seen enough TV crime shows to know a garment sprayed with Luminol will reveal bloodstains no matter how many times it is washed. The old jacket had to be disposed of in a spot so that it could never be found, and a dumpster wouldn't do. You always see cops rummaging through dumpsters in the TV detective shows. I wanted a permanent solution, one that would not keep me up at night worrying about incriminating evidence that could be located and identified.

As I drove to the mall thinking of the best way to dispose of the jacket a sudden thought came to me. Why was I going to a big box store to buy clothes? I never shopped in a discount store before so why now? All my purchases had been at local shops or at Brooks Bros. on the Miracle Mile in Manhasset. This was weird. Obviously my new entity is a bargain hunter. I wonder what he did for a living. For sure he didn't work on Wall Street.

After purchasing a new jacket I browsed the store and marveled at the fact that all the prices were discounted, all ridiculously inexpensive, and the quality of the merchandise, excellent. I wondered why I had never shopped at a discount store before, and I suddenly realized expensive stores were a rip off designed to inflate a person's ego with fawning salesman flashing saccharin smiles, and Catering to your every whim. The salesman probably laughed all the way to the bank. I could do without all that crap and from now on I would shop in stores that didn't make a fool of me.

My next stop was to the boat-launching ramp in Glen Cove. Glen Cove is a small city, about twenty-five miles from Manhattan, and adjacent to the town I live in. It's the center of the Long Island Gold Coast. Once you get out of the Glen Cove downtown area, and the few communities of sub-division homes, the entire area is rather rural and bucolic. Many home sites are on large tracts of land and you can still see a smattering of small farms, and horses grazing in their paddocks. Estates such as the Woolworth mansion still stand as a testament to the late 19th and early 20th century golden age, an age when the ultra rich fled the heat of the city to spend the summer in their "cottages", relaxing, partying, and sailing on Long Island Sound.

The boat ramp is located at the end of Garvies Point road. At one time, before Nassau County became a bedroom community for New York City, Garvies Point road was the center of the town's industrial base. Factories had access to the harbor, and trading ships plied the waters delivering their goods to international harbors. The area was a beehive of activity. Today though, the factories and commercial centers are abandoned, laid fallow by an accumulation of pollutants and industrial waste, the byproducts of years of unregulated industries, before government intervention. It's a toxic wasteland.

I entered the park, drove to the boat-launching ramp and parked my SUV next to the entrance of the ramp. I was the only one there. The parking lot was empty as I expected it to be this time of year and the area was void of boats, joggers or fisherman. After making sure I was alone I exited the car, rolled up the jacket, and dropped it into the water. The tide quickly carried it into the harbor and within a few minutes it disappeared under the waves. I washed my hands in the seawater and drove home, all the while thinking that I had done a good day's work, and deserved a nice cool martini.

***

Susan was not there when I returned home. She was probably at her sister's house unloading all of her troubles to a sympathetic ear, the troubles being yours truly. Having the house all to myself gave me the opportunity to carefully inspect my clothing and locate any overlooked blood evidence. But there was none. I was clean. It was if the day was like any other day, like nothing happened out of the ordinary.

Its amazing how one person can affect so many lives? In the time it takes to squeeze a trigger a life is gone. The hopes and aspirations the thief might have had before turning to drugs and crime, the joys he gave his parents when he was a child, the sorrows his mom felt when he never lived up to expectations are nothing but memories. The man whose life I took probably had a girlfriend who will grieve for him, and perhaps he left a child, now without a father, all gone in an instant.

On the other hand, my actions may have benefited society. The girlfriend may yet find a man who will be an honest responsible person who can be a father to a child and not destined to be a burden on society. And think of the money the state has saved. The thief would have ultimately been caught for some crime if I didn't snuff out his miserable life. I saved the state the expense of a trial and freed up a jail cell for a more worthy criminal. And think of all the potential muggings that I have been prevented, the lost saving of those who least could afford it.

I'm certain society will benefit from what was done, and I felt no remorse for the killing. What did concern me though was the callousness. Why didn't my conscience tell me that being a vigilante was not the way to solve a problem? Why did it feel like I did a good thing, and should be considered a hero, not a vicious villain? It is said that soldiers who kill in wartime or police who shoot a criminal in the line of duty feel regret and even have nightmares reliving the incident over and over. But I didn't think killing a thief and a scoundrel was going to cause me any loss of sleep. *What's wrong with me? Have I lost all feelings of remorse and compassion?*

***

There is definitely something wrong in my head. I have thoughts and emotions that are not normal, so bizarre that they can't even be talked about. And if I do something that's really crazy, and it becomes public knowledge I want my kids to read this and know that it's not my fault. I have to blame it on the Ouija spirit. But don't get me wrong. I don't mean to insinuate that I am about to commit any more murders. I think I have too much self-control for that. Killing the thief was unplanned, an act of self-defense. There was no other choice. His death was his fault, not mine.

Getting back to Susan's and my situation, I think I am going to have to leave her. Everything she does irritates me. For example, she will not even consider give up cigarettes even though she knows it annoys me. She cries over every little thing, and I didn't give a damn. Sometimes I get so angry I could strangle her. But I have too much self-control to do that, to kill her.

***

Susan burned dinner last night and it got me so pissed I hit her. It was the first time in my life I hit a woman, and I never even apologized when I cooled down. Actually I thought she deserved a slap on the face. Maybe next time she will keep an eye on the stove instead of wasting time reading the trashy harlequin novels she loves so much.

***

Susan and I had a hell of a fight. It started out with my taking a walk after breakfast. I had to get out of the house because Susan lit up a cigarette in the kitchen after our meal, while we were finishing our coffee. I know a smoke with coffee is sacrosanct because that used to be my favorite cigarette of the day. But she knows I can't stand the smell of them anymore and she either forgot that she should not smoke in my presence, or she is a just a hateful and stubborn bitch. Deep down inside I know she is not a hateful bitch, but just an old woman who is starting to get a bit of dementia. Nevertheless I had to get away from her, so I politely excused myself and told her I wanted to take a walk. I left the house feeling self-righteous and proud of myself for controlling my temper. But the good feeling didn't last long. Once on the street and alone with my active, restless mind, the good thoughts turned bad. *What the hell was I leaving the house for? She is the one who was in the wrong. God Damn it why am I still such a pussy? When I get back I'm going to see she gets her act together, or else.*

I continued to walk down our country lane. The sun was shinning, and the sky deep blue. It was a calm wind free day at street level but up above the telephone lines a light breeze stirred the branches of the tall trees causing them to shed their remaining leaves. The Maple trees, which lined the roadway, were the most impressive. Their leaves gave the appearance of golden flakes floating down from heaven. It was a perfect, brisk, November day. A day like this in the middle of an otherwise dreary season should have made me feel happy to be alive. It should have made me feel invigorated - but it did not. My thoughts began to grow darker and darker. I considered turning around and going home so that I could give Susan a piece of my mind, and not a good piece, that's for sure. But I kept walking, the pace increasing, and my mood growing darker with every step.

As I approached the Van Kamp's home I noticed that the summer flowers in the bed surrounding the mailbox were replaced with winter kale and cabbage, the ornamental kind, the ones with bright purple leaves, not the kind you eat.

Big shot has to show us how wealthy he is with all the fancy plantings. Just because his ancestors settled here a few hundred years ago he thinks he's special, fucking WASP bastard. I'll show him how special his gardens are. With that thought in mind I detoured off the road and trampled the flower bed and kicked a soccer ball sized cabbage's off its stem and into the front lawn. I wanted to make sure he knew that it was not just a car that had drifted off the road and into his cabbage patch.

That will show the pompous bastard what I think of his plantings and his money.

I left the Van Kamp's property dragging my feet to mess up the decorative mulch covering the flower bed and continued walking down the road when suddenly a golf ball appeared out of nowhere. It skipped across the street and hit me in the leg before I could get out of the way. I looked up and scanned the surroundings. On the far side of the street, the north side, I saw the culprit, the person responsible for the errant golf ball. It was a black kid, about twenty years old, the son of a dentist who lived on the block, and he was wielding a sand wedge, a club used for very short distances. He must have topped the ball because it certainly should not have traveled into the street.

"Hey boy what the fuck you doing hitting golf balls at me," I said.

He immediately stiffened up. His face turned into a scowl. I could see he didn't like my use of the word "boy". It's like using the "N' word. But I didn't give a damn.

When his family moved into the neighborhood several of my neighbors went into an uproar. We all had multi-million dollar homes and even though the new owner was a successful businessman owning a few dental clinics some of us still didn't like the idea of a black family living in our neighborhood and possibly dragging down the property values. At the time I seem to recall that I stood up for the family. I figured if he had the money what the hell was the difference. There wasn't much of a chance that the average black family would be able to afford anything on the street. But that was then and this is now. Then I was a bleeding heart liberal, now I don't know what I am, but I know that my pussy days are a thing of the past.

I didn't let it rest, "You could fit a football field in your backyard. Why the hell are you hitting balls out by the street?"

He was getting angry, but he kept his temper.

"It's really none of your business." he replied, "But if you must know, I'm waiting for the mail to be delivered. There is something coming that requires my immediate attention."

"Yeah, sure, does your pusher mail your drugs instead of hand delivering them?"

I could see his temper was rising. If he wasn't so black his face would probably have been beet red with anger.

"There's no cause for that kind of talk mister."

"I'll talk any God damned way I want to."

"I don't have to listen to this kind of crap either."

And with that statement he turned his back on me and started to walk away, back to his house. This got me angrier. Nobody turns his back on me and gets away with it. I was just getting started.

"Hey, I'm not through talking to you. Why the hell aren't you at work doing something productive? Think if you keep hitting golf balls and endangering people's lives you will be another Tiger Woods?"

He didn't answer; he just kept walking.

"Well fuck you." I said, as I picked up the ball lying in the road "And don't leave without your fucking golf ball either."

I picked up the golf ball and threw it with all the energy I could muster, not at the young man who was nearing the front door of his home, but at the front bay window of his house. It was a big target and impossible to miss. The glass shattered into a thousand pieces and when the tinkling sound of glass shards ended I smiled at the dumbstruck youth, turned on my heels and headed towards my home, never looking back.

That will teach the black bastard to mess with me.

When I reached my house I expected to see patrol cars with flashing lights parked at our driveway, and the police waiting at our doorstep, but everything was peaceful and quiet, just as it should be in our quiet village. I smiled to myself as I hummed the old Weavers hit song, The Lion Sleeps Tonight. *In the village, the peaceful village, the lion sleeps tonight,*

But when I reached the front door of my home, my little village, it was not so peaceful. Susan was pacing the vestibule floor just waiting for me and she exploded when the door opened.

"What the hell is going on? Are you crazy? Whatever made you break the Washington's window?"

I guess Mrs. Washington called our house. How did she get our number? It's unlisted. Does Susan have friends I don't know about? Is she having a ménage a' trios with the Washington's? Maybe that's why she's an iceberg in bed lately?

"Well their son is a nut job. He drove a golf ball at me."

"That's not true and you know it. I'm sure it was purely unintentional, an accident. Are you getting completely crazy?"

Now that's something I didn't want to hear. I'm not crazy and I get angry at statements like that.

"The young bastard has a back yard. He should use it for dangerous activities."

"Since when is golf considered a dangerous sport?"

"Well what's done is done. Fuck them; I'm going upstairs to my office."

"You know it's going to cost the best part of a thousand dollars to replace the window."

"They can go to hell. I'm not giving them a dime. Let them sue me."

"I'm sure they will, and you're getting to be an embarrassment in the neighborhood. I can hardly face my friends anymore with all the fighting and goings on here. You think the neighbors don't know how you changed? Louise was at the supermarket when we had that fight over the crock pot and she told Nancy, and I'm sure everyone knows about it by now."

Susan lit a fuse. She was going where she should not have gone and I was starting to see red. I started up the stairs. I had to get away from Susan, but she wouldn't leave me alone. She kept up the barrage. I took the stairs two steps at a time. I had to get away. I ran to my office. My head was spinning, both from the exertion of running up the stairs and from the rise of my blood pressure. I couldn't see very clearly, my vision was blurred, but somehow I managed to navigate to the office closet to retrieve the shotgun. I picked up the weapon, chambered a round, and ran back to the head of the stairs. I raised the gun to a waist high position, my left hand on the stock, my right hand on the grip, index finger on the trigger, and the barrel pointed at Susan's head.

"Shut the fuck up or I'll blow you to hell where you belong, you bitch."

We both stood frozen in time, Susan too terrified to run and I, well thinking about it now, I don't know what I thought. Violent images raced through my mind but now that I try to recall them they are as nebulous as last weeks dream. I just stood there – a zombie wanting to kill, to tear flesh, to see limbs being torn from bodies, to see eviscerated entrails, and watch bloody gore spill to the floor. It was a horrific moment that ended when Susan finally let out an ear splitting scream and bolted from the vestibule and into the kitchen, a place that offered her a sense of security and sanity.

After a while, I don't know for how long, I returned the shotgun to my office closet and went downstairs. My anger was spent, and I felt remorse for what I had done, and I haven't felt sorry for causing Susan pain in a long time.

When I entered the kitchen I found Susan sitting on a chair, her head resting on folded arms on the tabletop. She was sobbing ever so softly, drained of energy. It seemed to me her vitality, her youthful spirit, and her very life had been sapped away never to return. Between violent gut shaking sobs she whispered,

"I can't take it any more, God help me -- I can't take it any more." And I had no reply.

****

The situation is getting bad, real bad. Susan and I argue and fight all the time now. I figure I'll have to leave before she divorces me, or I kill her. I really don't have a choice. Divorce is out of the question. It's too expensive and complicated, and I'd get the short end of it. I'll just leave. I'll withdraw half our savings and disappear. The money should last for the little time I have left and I could always find a part time job if I had to. Of course I would have to get a job that pays in cash since I couldn't report earnings to social security least they track me down, so I would have to forfeit my monthly SSI check. But one has to make a few sacrifices for a new life, and I don't get that much money from the government anyway. I'm sure Susan will be OK. She runs the family business and gets a salary; the house is paid for, and I won't empty the bank account. I'll miss the kids, but I could call them once in a while using a prepaid cell phone. After all, if it wasn't for Ouija I would be dead from the cancer, and out of their life altogether. Sometimes you have to take the bad with the good and make the best of it. I'll write and remind them of that.

November 16th

Well I did it. I took the bull by the horns and started to pave my way to a new life. It will take a few weeks to get it all together, but what I did was a start and there is no going back. I secretly sold a little over half our stocks and bonds, withdrew the money, and put it into an online bank account. I had to use my social security number to open the account but I figure it will be at least six months or more before the government or Susan catches up with me. By that time I will be settled in another state or maybe in a south sea island in the Pacific. Tahiti would be nice. From what I hear it's a nice place to live. Maybe I can take up painting like Paul Gauguin. There are lovely young brown skin girls in bikini bathing suits lounging on the beach, and crystal clear ocean waters to swim and sail in. What more could a guy my age ask for? But whatever I do and wherever I live at least Susan and the so-called friends who drive me crazy with their unsolicited advice will be out of my life. I'm not worried, I'll figure out what to do. Of course a new identity will be the first priority. The online bank account will have to be closed and converted to cash or into gold bullion or collectable coins. Gold appreciates much faster than interest on money in the bank. Everything should be okay.

December 8th

The few weeks before I left was a trying time. I stayed on through Thanksgiving for the kids' sake. They don't have the foggiest idea things are not quite right in our once happy household. Hard as it was, I held my temper during their long weekend stay with us, and Susan and I were on our best behavior. Outside of those few days we hardly ever talk to each other. As I said earlier, she is an optimist, an ostrich with her head in the ground, and naive to boot. I'm sure she blames my temper and bad moods an aftereffect of the cancer scare and that I would return to normal in time. But she is wrong; I don't think I'll ever be the person I once was. What she does not understand is that my anger is not a temporary condition. In fact it's getting worse, and the uncontrollable rage I feel is affecting all aspects of my life, including relationships with friends.

***

I used to play doubles tennis every Sunday morning with the same group of friends, and the game has been unbroken for the past twenty years. But a few weeks after the Ouija cure I dropped out of the group for good because some of the men cheat, and I lost my temper over a bad call one of my opponents made. I knew the guy could see where the ball landed, but after a long rally, which I should have won, he called "out" when it was obvious the ball was "in". For Christ sake the ball left a mark on the outer line tape. He had to see it. I blew my cork and my teammates didn't back me up when I challenged the call. Let them all go to hell. I didn't need their crap, and I didn't need the game.

Another incident that took all my self-control to keep from going ballistic was when I thought I might bash in a guy's head with a tire iron. I was sitting at a red light and this jerk crashed his car into mine. It was only a fender bender but it was clearly the other driver's fault. He was talking on his cell phone and not paying attention.

Immediately after being hit I relocated my car boxing in the other driver's vehicle so he could not leave the scene of the accident. I got out of the car and stormed over to the drivers side of the other guy's car and shouted,

"You dumb ass-hole, why the fuck don't you watch where you're going."

The driver rolled down his window to answer me, but taken by surprise he neglected to put his cell phone down. He was still holding it up to his right ear. Infuriated by his lack of concern I reached over his chest, grabbed the phone, and threw it as far as I could. It landed hard on the road in front of us and the plastic case splintered into little shards. The guts of the phone, the battery and little pieces of metal slid down the asphalt. *I hope it's an expensive I Phone you ass hole.*

The driver turned beet red in anger. His eyebrows shot up and his jaw dropped. He sat motionless for a moment, shocked, not believing his eyes, and then reacted. I never saw a person unhook a seat belt and get out of a car so fast. The other driver was no victim, not by a long shot, and I respected him for that. He bolted out of his car ready to do battle. I was startled for a moment, as young men usually don't want to go to war with old guys like me. But my adversary was really angry, and my adrenalin must also have been flowing because I dashed back to my car, retrieved a tire iron stored under the driver's seat, and faced my opponent. We stood there face to face, two gladiators ready to battle to the death, I with the tire iron held high, and he with closed fists ready to strike.

"What the hell is the matter with you, are you nuts or something?" he shouted.

Calling me "nuts" always sets me off, and I was beginning to lose it.

"You and the damned cell phone; why don't you just look where you're going and keep the God damned phone in your pocket."

"Well the phone cost me $240.00 and you're going to pay for it."

"Like hell I am."

"We'll see about that. I'm going to shove that tire iron up your ass if I don't get my money."

"Bull shit and you can fix the car's hood too."

With that statement I stepped over to the front of his car and smashed the tire iron into the car's hood leaving a two-inch dent.

The guy was big, young, and physically fit. I didn't stand a chance. He charged me like an infuriated bull after a Picador had stuck a lance into its hide, and I immediately went down landing hard on my back. He then straddled my prostrate body and began choking the life out of me. I think the big guy would have succeeded in killing me if it wasn't for a few pedestrians who stopped to see what the ruckus was all about. The good Samaritans separated us and I got to my feet while the brute was held back. But while they were trying to calm the man down I got into my car and sped away before anyone could stop me.

While driving away from the accident I thought about the incident. I think one of the bystanders got my license plate number so I'm sure I will get a call from the police before long. I only hoped it would be in a week or two before the cops located me, and maybe I would be long gone by then. I also realized my revenge, the breaking of the man's phone, was a controlled reaction. I had not lost control, and never went ballistic. If I had really gone bonkers I probably would have bashed in the man's head and not just the car's hood. My actions were controlled. It was just my anger boiling over, nothing else. Besides, the guy deserved it. Using a hand held cell phone is against the law and he broke the law. It was as though I was making a citizen's arrest. I was just the judge, jury, and enforcer.

The government should ban the Goddamned cell phones altogether. It's another useless gadget the world can do without. One day they will find out it fries your brain. Who is going to pay for the doctor bills then? You can bet your sweet ass it will be the taxpayer, not the phone company.

December 17th

The anxiety caused by the anticipation of the police knocking at my door over the latest road rage incident, the fights with Susan, and the dark winter days in Locust Valley were getting too much for me to handle any longer. So I packed my Nissan with some bare necessities, and the shotgun, and took off for Florida. It was the perfect opportunity as Susan and her girlfriend had taken the train into the city for a day of shopping. I can't even imagine what she must have thought when she got home and read my farewell note. Of course I was a gentleman and blamed all our troubles on myself. Aside from that not being the truth, that it was my fault, gentlemen always take the *mea culpa* route to ease the shock of a break up.

***

Florida is called the sunshine state, and I hope with good reason, because I surely needed some sunshine in my life. I had memories of good times in South Florida and that's why I chose it for my new home. In the past, once the children could be left alone, Susan and I vacationed in the Ft. Lauderdale area every January at a time-share we owned. It was a nice resort directly on the ocean, with a white sand beach, and lush landscaping consisting of flowering shrubs and tall palm trees that provided shade when the sun got to be too hot. There was a thatched Tiki bar that served generous man-sized drinks for a reasonable price, and the resort played never-ending Calypso music.

When you sit on a reclining lounge chair with the gentle waves lapping at your feet, and a cool rum punch in your hand, life is wonderful. You feel as if you were vacationing on a Caribbean island without the threat of getting mugged by the local natives.

Part 2 – Florida

December 20th

The drive to my new home took three days. I took my time, stopping off at a few local attractions, and watering holes. One of the interesting attractions was the legendary Fountain of Youth in St. Augustine. Everyone thinks the explorer Ponce de Leon was searching for a magical fountain to regain his youth when in actuality he was only seeking a cure for his impotence. At least that is what Gonzalo Fernandez de Oviedo's states in his 1535 history book. And we always think women are the catty ones.

But to get back to more serious matters, as I motored down I-95 I was excited and looked forward to moving into an apartment near the resort Susan and I had previously vacationed at, in the town of Pompano Beach. However my elevated mood didn't last long. When I arrived at the beach area I discovered the rents were totally outrageous. I had no idea inflation had driven prices up so much that the town had become a playground for the very rich. Among other things, what is wrong with this country is that everything worthwhile is for the rich bastards. They control the world.

***

I took a fleabag motel off A1A for the night after being frustrated by being unable to find, or afford a decent apartment by the beach, and the next morning headed south, ending up in Kendel, a town ten miles south of Miami. It's a residential community for those who work in the city and I chose that suburb because the rentals were plentiful and cheap. Unemployment is at record levels in Dade County and it is reflected in the large inventory of empty apartments. The unit I chose was so nondescript it's not worth mentioning. But it was furnished, and for the time being that was all I needed until I could get my head straight and my act together. After the winter vacation season I planned to move north and sublet a snowbird's vacant apartment. Rents are always less out of season in Broward County and especially if you stayed out of the ocean beach area.

May 8th

I keep burning bridges and for the life of me I don't know why. True, things are not as I expected them to be, and it makes me angry, and my anger gets me into trouble, so I guess that's the reason. It's frustrating knowing I can't afford a really nice place in Palm Beach County. However there are plenty of nice communities in Broward, and I did expect to live in that county and be happy. Unfortunately, to my surprise, I discovered that even Broward was out of my financial means. But having to live in Kendel, now that's really the pit's. After all, I worked hard all my life to be able to afford the better things in life, a nice house, a boat, membership in an upscale tennis club, one with a country club atmosphere, things like that. I could have forked over the big bucks for membership in a country club, one with outrageous membership bonds, fees, and mandatory restaurant commitments, but golf sucks in my book -- too slow a game, so I choose not to join a club -- but I could afford it. That's the point. And I did have all the amenities money can buy, all the material things, the things which separates me from the masses, the proletariat. I've become accustomed to living the good life so it really hurts when I have to live like a country hick, a redneck trailer trash hillbilly.

There I go again, getting off subject. I started off by saying that I keep burning bridges and I want to explain what I mean. To be on the record – firstly what happened in the pool hall was not my fault; it's the damn Cuban immigrants who started the whole damn thing.

Last week boredom was really kicking in and I decided to get out of the house and do something other than watching a dumb movie at a local flea bitten theatre, and it had to be something I could do by myself. I don't have any friends in Kendal, nor did I want any. The local residents are all low class people. Not "low class" by the federal government statistics, not economically poor that is. I suppose most of them are hard working middle class folks, but not the kind of people I'm accustomed to socializing with. The locals think a big recreational day on the weekend is a backyard barbeque with hot dogs and burgers. Or they might go fishing in one of the canals, or off a pier. It's not that I'm against fishing. There was nothing better than going out on my boat in the wee hours of the morning, when the sun was just rising and the tide turning, and jigging for a big stripe bass. Now that's fishing. But the hillbillies here think fishing for a six inch bony pigfish is sport and worth catching, and for God's sake, even eating. Don't they know it's only a fish used for bait to catch real fish? They can go to a bait shop and just buy the filthy things, pan fry them and use the bones for toothpicks.

But to get back to the bridge burning, I was bored and didn't want to see a movie and my budget didn't allow for chartering a boat for some deep sea fishing, so I went to a local pool hall. My ex-tennis club had a billiards table in the clubhouse and I have been known to be a good pool player, even by some accounts, a pool shark. I thought picking up a scratch game might also be a way to have some fun and at the same time pick up some extra spending money.

And so I left my little dingy apartment after a crappy TV dinner of fried chicken, mashed potatoes and string beans, and walked the few blocks to the neighborhood Pollo Loco Bar and Grill, a run down seedy joint that capitalizes on the franchised restaurant's name, "El Pollo Loco". When I entered the so-called eatery my first thought was: perhaps I should notify the real restaurant franchiser and tell them of the name infringement. The place was an embarrassment, and should be shut down, and I might get a finder's fee for whistle blowing. But I quickly dismissed the thought. I'm not a squealer, never have been, and never will be.

As I said, the place was seedy. The floor was filthy with beer stains making for visible footprints in front of, and around the bar stools. The once white ceiling was yellowed indicating decades of dust and stale cigarette smoke, and the dark paneled walls once shiny were dulled and streaked with grime. I don't know why they called the place a restaurant, as there were no tables. If you wanted to have a meal it was served at the bar, and the menu was limited to Spanish fare, pre-cooked taquitos, burritos, tacos and some other Spanish crap, certainly not a suitable restaurant for Americans from Locust Valley, or at least not for this American. In retrospect the TV dinner was not so bad after all.

I sat down at the end of the bar, the end closest to the front door being careful not to allow my elbows to contact the bar's greasy counter top (no telling what diseases might be harbored on it) and ordered a bottle of Corona. Who knows what was in the draft beer; no sense in taking chances. I also told the barkeep to skip the glass. Drinking out of the bottle was just fine for me, once again, why take chances. I had to shout out the order to the bartender as he was at the other end of the bar watching a soccer game on TV, a pre-recorded game from Spain. Soccer is a passion here with the immigrant wetbacks. The Corona was fetched from an open tub filled with ice, opened, and a slice of lime inserted into the bottle, and unceremoniously slid down the length of the bar coming to rest right in front of me. I was impressed. The barkeep could have been a shuffleboard champ.

What I was not impressed with however was the squeezing of a lime into my beer bottle. The bartender probability didn't wash his hands all day. He probably took a crap in the bathroom and didn't wash his hands afterwards, and he more than likely picked his nose to boot. I was starting to get a little pissed, but held my temper. After all, I was in the place for some fun and maybe a little extra pocket cash.

I downed half a beer and moseyed down to the far end of the bar; the area devoted to the pool table, and watched a foursome play 8 ball. Very unorthodox in my neck of the woods to shoot pool with four people but since there was only one pool table I suppose adjustments had to be made. The men shot three rounds while I sat at the end barstool quietly drinking my Corona and observing the play. Jesus Christ, what a bunch of amateurs. At the end of the games, the losing team paid the winners and I suppose there had been many games played because several hundred dollars passed between them. A brisk conversation ensued and the four men garbled something in Spanish for a few minutes. Afterwards the two winners and one of the losers moved over to the bar for some refreshment. This left only one man of the losing team left at the table, and he came over to me and asked if I wanted to play. The stakes were $10.00 a round. The bet was within my budget and besides I didn't figure on losing.

The first round went my way and I won with three of his balls remaining on the table. We split the next two games and he won the next game, but not by much. We were now even, he winning two games and I won two.

By this time I had consumed a few beers and was feeling a bit cocky. My shots had been steadily improving after such a long hiatus from the game, and I knew I could take him.

"Want to make this a real game?" I said.

"Sure boss, what's your pleasure?" he replied

"I don't know, how about doubling it to $20.00 a game."

"Sure boss, anything you say, I'll rack 'em up."

He racked them and I had the first shot. It was a good break and the number eleven ball went into the end pocket. This gave me a great advantage. I ran the next three balls before missing a shot and relinquishing my turn thus leaving only three balls to sink before going for the eight ball and winning the game. Then it was my opponent's turn. He ran three and scratched. I still had a definite advantage. We parried about for a while, sometimes sinking a ball and sometimes shooting a safety. But in the end I won the game.

It was now my turn to rack them and he went first. He had a great break and ran a few balls and then I ran a few. However in the end he beat me with only one of my balls remaining on the table.

We played a few more games and his game improved rapidly, more so than mine, and as I said, I had gotten back into the groove and should have been way ahead in games, but I was not. It was starting to get me angry. I think I was snookered into playing with a hustler.

The next game was his turn to rack, and mine to break. He did the honors while I went to the men's room, and then to the bar for another beer. When I came back to the table the rack had been set so I took a big gulp of the Corona, chalked the cue stick and slammed the cue ball into the rack. I expected to see an explosion of balls in every direction. But that was not what happened. The noise was the giveaway. Normally you would hear a sharp report then the cue ball connected with a tight, properly set rack of balls, but the sound was a dull thud. The balls did not scatter, as they should have. Obviously the first ball was not tight against the number two and three. It was a bad rack and it must have been done intentionally. Only a rank amateur could have made such a mistake, and this guy was no amateur by any stretch of the imagination.

While the balls on the pool table did not explode, as they should have, I did. I went totally bonkers. Without a moment's hesitation I flipped the cue stick into the air and caught it by the shaft, the ferrule end, and swung the butt of the stick at my opponent's head. He was caught completely off guard. He never saw it coming and didn't even flinch. The butt hit him squarely in the temple and he went down as in a feint, like a silent movie heroine who swoons upon learning of her lover's death.

The man's friends, his buddies at the bar, the ones who had played pool earlier watched the entire incident and sprang into action. The three of them charged me, fists clenched ready for a bar room brawl. But their mistake was that being in such haste the men never armed themselves, and a fist is no match for a long club-like weapon. I spun 90 degrees and faced the men like a baseball player at home plate ready for a fastball or a slider, or anything a pitcher might throw at him. When the first guy got in range I let him have it with all the strength I could muster. Luckily my new entity was left-handed so the butt of the stick caught him above the right shoulder, and he was out of the action with a busted collarbone. Unfortunately the cue stick broke with the impact of the first strike and I was left holding a two-foot splinter of wood. The cue stick was useless as a club.

On the other hand I suppose it was fortunate the cue stick broke as I had no room to swing a club because the second guy was all over me in an instant. He knocked me to the ground and pinned my left arm, my bicep muscle to the floor. But I still had mobility in my forearm and able to use the splinter of wood as a weapon, a short pointed stabbing sword. Good thing I remembered the Romans conquered the world using a short sword and not a cumbersome slicing weapon, and that's the kind of soldier I would emulate. Using just my lower forearm I attempted to thrust the sharp splinter into the guy's gut. However the plan was not entirely successful. I would have skewered him like a piece of meat on a Shish Kabob but it didn't turn out that way. All I was able to do was to impale him through the fleshy part of his midsection, his love handle. It would be a long time before his girlfriend could take a hold of that part of his body when he screwed her.

The next thing I remember was lying on the ground in a fetal position, curled up like a baby in the womb, desperately trying to protect my face and groin area from the fierce kicks of the remaining man who was still standing untouched and unscathed. What the hell, taking out two of the three was not bad for a guy like me. You can't win them all.

At long last, after what seemed to be an eternity, but in actuality was only a minute or two, the kicking stopped. The man who was trying to separate my head from my torso was being held back by another bar patron giving me time to get to my feet. I stumbled up, wobbly and weaving, trying to get my eyes to focus and to make it to the door, to get the hell out of there as fast as I could, but I was stopped by the man who broke up the fight.

"Not so fast, tough guy," he said, "I saw the whole thing. You started it."

"Well the guy set me up. He cheated." I said.

"Hey, there are some better ways to settle an argument. You could have killed someone and as it is Roberto needs an ambulance."

"Is he okay? I didn't mean to hurt him but they were attacking me." I said sheepishly.

Like hell, give me another chance and I'll kill him.

"That's a lot of bull shit, and you know it. You slammed the cue stick into Jose's head without him even seeing it coming. His brains could be all over the floor. What the hell were you thinking? Think his friends would not be there to help? Let's go wise guy, I'm calling the cops."

With that statement the barkeeper grabbed me and twisted my right arm behind my back. For the moment I was helpless. I considered kicking the barkeep in the balls and making a run for it, but I was still so dizzy I could hardy stand up no less run, so I thought perhaps I could talk my way out of the situation. Thankfully though, it didn't come to that. Roberto spoke up; he was the guy I stabbed.

"Sam, let him go. It's only a flesh wound. I'll see doc, he'll fix me up. I can't take a chance and go to the hospital. The cops still have a warrant out for me. I can't risk it"

Wow, what luck. Maybe I can still talk my way out of this.

"Look guys, I'm really sorry for all this. I really didn't mean it. Sometimes I lose my temper, that's all. Here, I've got almost $100.00 in my wallet. Take it. It will pay for doc to take care of the wound, and once again, I'm sorry."

Sorry, my ass, I just wish I could have killed all of you.

Roberto took the money and Sam gave me a few parting words,

"You got off easy mister. But if I ever see you in here again I'll drive my foot so far up your ass you'll be eating shit cakes for a week. Now get the fuck out of here, and don't ever come back."

They didn't have to tell me twice. I left before one of them changed his mind and I went straight home. I did not pass "go" and did not collect one hundred dollars. Life is a monopoly game. You roll the dice every day and sometimes it comes out big time, and sometimes not.

***

When I entered my apartment I poured myself a big scotch - straight up, and flopped into the crummy threadbare easy chair that came with the shitty little rental. I sipped the drink and replayed the entire night through my mind. "Once again the local punks almost fucked up my life. If the cops nabbed me it would have been all over. I really have to learn to control my temper, even when it's somebody else's fault, like what happened tonight. But I got the best of them. It only cost me $100.00 and I probably would be in to the snookering bastard for much more than that. Now who has the last laugh?"

With that final thought, I finished my drink and went to the bathroom to see why I tasted blood in my mouth. The mirror told it all. There was a gash over my right eye and the taste of blood was from the tooth that was knocked out. My chest hurt like hell when I breathed so I supposed there might be a couple of cracked ribs to contend with. I looked into the mirror again and a sudden thought, an old joke came to me. The patient says, "Doctor, it hurts when I laugh", the doctor replies, "so don't laugh." But I did laugh into the mirror. It was all worth it. The only thing that really bothered me was the broken tooth. I'll have to see a dentist about that. But even that is okay. When I get the invoice I'll tear it up and find another dentist - if I ever need one.

**

I finally moved from Kendel. Things weren't so great there, too many Latino foreigners. The Cuban population is huge in South Florida and has been for quite a while, ever since Batista was overthrown and Fidel Castro assumed power back in 1959. And now there is a growing influx of Haitians from the Caribbean. But worst of all are the wetbacks up from Mexico and Central America. The entire area below Ft. Lauderdale is overwhelmingly Spanish and the immigrants get on my nerves. They are not like the Europeans who passed through Ellis Island in the early 20th Century. They don't have any intention of assimilating or becoming American citizens, and they won't even try to learn our language. For Christ sake if they want to live in this country they should at the very least learn to speak English. To make matters worse Florida caters to them to such an extent they will never bother to learn our language. Street signs are in Spanish, restaurant menus are in Spanish; even the application for a driver's license is in Spanish. What really made me laugh though is a sign at a neighborhood restaurant named, "The New York Steakhouse". A sign on the front window reads, "English spoken here". I couldn't wait to get the hell out of town and to get back into the real America.

June 22nd

It is hot as hell and summer isn't even here yet. I moved from Kendel to the Florida West coast, to St. Petersburg, partly because I couldn't take the large

Spanish population in Dade County, and because I thought it would be cooler up north. But I was mistaken; people in Pinellas County tell me that it can get hot as hell in the summer, just like Miami. And I'm finding out that the locals are right; it is getting hot, and even worse is the humidity. Maybe that's why you never see ads for Saunas; who needs them? All you have to do for a good hot steam bath is to walk outside. There is always a good side to everything though, and the good side of the unrelenting heat is that the homeless do not need a hot plate to fry eggs. They can use the sidewalks.

I rejected moving into a sublet, as they are for the most part condos, which the snowbirds use for the winter season. Come springtime they move back north to their permanent residence for the summer so they can visit and aggravate their children, and spoil their grandchildren. The few remaining retirees who can't afford to go north are crotchety seniors who stick their nose into everyone's business. I cannot take that kind of crap so I rejected a low cost sublet and rented a furnished apartment. Maybe if I ever decide to stay in one place long enough I'd get a real apartment buy some furniture and settle down. But for now having roots in a community is for trees and shrubs, not for me.

The building I finally settled on is an eight-unit garden apartment with my unit located on the first floor facing the pool. The complex is nice enough. It's in a blue-collar working class neighborhood close to a shopping center, and the interstate extension.

The apartment has one bedroom, a living room with sliding glass doors opening onto a small balcony, a kitchenette and one bathroom with a shower – no tub. That's enough for me though, "simple is better" That's my new motto. I don't want to spend time maintaining rooms that would never be occupied.

My neighbors are for the most part singles and working couples without children. It's quiet with no little kids or crying babies to get my temper up. Best of all everyone minds their own business. They are too busy just trying to make a living.

***

My day passes something like this: Up at 8:00AM, shower, get dressed, fix a cup of coffee without an accompanying cigarette, and drink it on the patio. Coffee is not as enjoyable since I quit smoking. I guess my new entity never smoked, and once he (or it) entered my body I found the habit disgusting. But my body must still have a deep hidden residual memory of the pleasure of a cigarette with a cup of coffee, and I occasionally crave a smoke. Old habits die hard.

After coffee I usually walk to the supermarket to get the newspaper, the St. Petersburg Times, come home, and read it cover to cover. Then it's into the pool for a few laps to get a little exercise and to loosen up the worn out muscles and joints. Afterwards I stretch out on a lounge chair in the patio area to soak up some sun until I get bored.

Incidentally, it doesn't take long for me to get bored. That's another personality quirk Ouija gave me. Eventually when the glaring sun reaches its zenith and signals lunchtime I head back to my apartment, fix a sandwich, and take another shower. If they ever need a poster boy for Mr. Clean the ad agencies can look me up. After the shower I surf the Internet and check on the stocks that were once in my portfolio, making note that I am better off in gold coins. At least they hold their value and not tank like the stock market did. Won't this recession ever end? At 6:00 it's suppertime. (If you can call a frozen TV dinner food.) When the ersatz meal is finished with most of it winding up in the garbage I might read a book for a while, and it's usually a very "short while" as my concentration is not what it used to be. Then I watch TV for an hour or two, and it's off to sleep, either on the couch or in my bed.

****

I'm going crazy with boredom, and getting angry again for no reason. I thought that when I relocated to Florida, lived a quiet peaceful existence, and had no stress, life would be different, be better. But it is not so. I'm settled in my new home and finished with the move yet I'm still tormented with anger and restlessness. Moving out of New York accomplished nothing. The only saving grace is I left Locust Valley before killing Susan.

July 16th

A new tenant moved into the complex a week ago and he is getting on my nerves. I have a very strange feeling our fates are intertwined somehow, that his destiny is going to coincide with mine someday, so I think he should be mentioned in my diary. I don't know what the future holds for us but somehow he is going to change the path of my life, and likewise I think his life will be altered as well. Maybe my new entity knows what our future holds, but he is not telling.

The new occupant is a man in his mid twenties. He doesn't work, and often gets to the swimming pool before me. He lounges at the pool for hours on end sitting in the shade under the single palm tree, my favorite spot. That pisses me off. While we've had many opportunities to get acquainted and say "hello", we haven't done so. He, like me, is a loner and doesn't connect with any of the other tenants. The guy is white, about six feet tall, has a gaunt face with a straggly goatee, and thin as a rail. I don't think he has eaten a solid meal in ages or consumed any solid food, as I never see him bring groceries home from the supermarket. But he does drink copious amounts of beer and smokes weed in public. It's possible he is an ex-con as he has a tattoo of a knife on the inside of his left forearm, and on his right bicep, a large swastika with a cross, and indicating membership in a white supremacist gang.

He is a prime example of the worst kind of trailer trash, and I have taken an instant dislike to him.

July 21st, 10:00 AM

Something is definitely not kosher with our new tenant. He exits the apartment complex on Tuesdays and Fridays, leaving in the evening at about 8:30PM carrying a small package, and he usually returns around midnight empty handed. My curiosity has been piqued and I plan on following him when he goes out at night to find out what he is up to. I have a feeling he is not going to church, or volunteering at a soup kitchen. Maybe he is a Cub Scout leader and going to a meeting where he could fondle some young boys. I wouldn't put anything past him, the creep.

July 21st, 11:30 PM

I just got home from an evening out and feeling great, no anxiousness, and no anger, just a feeling of contentment knowing I finally have something to do, some purpose for my life, a mission, and it concerns the new neighbor. The feeling of our coming together is about to come true.

I left the apartment a few minutes before 8:00 PM this evening and drove down our street to the first traffic light, parked my Nissan SUV fifty yards before the light and waited for the new tenant's arrival. He had to pass by my car to get out of the neighborhood, and I didn't have long to wait. His car appeared in the rear view mirror a few minutes after 8:30 coming up the street right on schedule. When he passed me I started the Nissan and followed at a discreet distance behind his car. He turned right at the intersection and proceeded down the boulevard for about a mile. Fortunately the traffic was light enough so it was possible for me to remain far enough behind him so my vehicle would not be spotted. When he made a left turn I continued traveling down the road for a few blocks and then went home. I wasn't going to trail him too closely and risk being recognized. Rome wasn't built in a day. There was no rush. He would be making the same trip again and eventually I would be there to see his ultimate destination, and to discover the purpose of his journey. I bet it's for some illegal reason.

July 24th

Once again, I left the apartment a few minutes before 8:00 PM, drove to the spot where I ended the tail the other day, parked the car pointing in the direction the new tenant would be traveling, shut off the engine and waited for him to arrive.

Everyone needs a handle, so for future reference, and since he is tall and lanky, I named the new guy "Stretch". Sure enough, within fifteen minutes he came into view. When he passed I started up the SUV and followed him. After a few blocks and a few turns I was ready to call it a day as following someone for too long is a sure way to be spotted. But before I was able to cut short the surveillance Stretch pulled over to the curb and parked his car a few feet from a neighborhood bar and grill. There were only two buildings on the street, a bar with an unusual name of "The Green Lizard" and a Laundromat. Since Stretch did not have a laundry bag in his hand it had to be assumed he was headed for the local watering hole. I knew the next time he would be at the bar so I didn't stop but kept driving and went home.

July 29th

Yesterday was the day I found out why Stretch makes his scheduled runs. He could have been selling bootleg cigarettes, or stolen watches, or ladies cosmetics for all I knew. But the odds were that his merchandise was something that could not be sold over a counter in a department store. So I drove to the Green Lizard getting there well before Stretch's anticipated arrival to find out if my assumptions were correct.

It was a nice enough bar and grill although the management must have not heard about the Florida smoking ban in dining areas, or more likely they could care less. Most likely they give the local cop a free lunch so he would look the other way.

After cutting my way through the haze I sat in the last free table facing the bar in the dining section of the restaurant and eyeballed the place. The room was dark, the only source of light coming from low candlepower sconce fixtures. The bar area was done in mahogany, very classy in its day but a little tired now. The wall behind the bar was mirrored with shelving to hold and display the inventory of liquor bottles. The middle of the mirrored wall was free of shelving and in the vacant space was displayed a giant green three foot long Iguana. When I first saw the bar I wondered why they named the place the "Green Lizard" and not something nautical like "The Moorings", or the "Crusty Anchor", since the town is known for boating and water activities. Maybe the proprietors thought a reptilian name for the restaurant might attract South American clientele. They eat lizards, and perhaps a patron might have assumed an Iguana would be featured on the menu.

The decorations in the dining area consisted of photographs of bikers and boxers. Jake "the Raging Bull" LaMotta, and Jack Dempsey were on the wall along with an 8x10 highlighted autographed photo of Rocky Graziano. Other photographs showed bikers circling a track or kicking up dirt on a motto-cross track. A crack on one of the picture frames, and a few scratched chairs indicated that the establishment might have been be a good place to have a bar room fight. In spite of the obvious deficiencies the pub and restaurant was doing a fair amount of business.

There were six men at the bar and one very tired looking woman well past her prime trying to look sexy by making goo-goo eyes at one of the guys standing at the bar. She looked desperate for someone to foot the bill for her drinks, and I suppose for someone to share her bed that night. At the far end of the building there were a rowdy group of wannna-be bikers shooting pool and drinking beer. They had the requisite leather jackets but no bikes parked outside. The dining area was also doing a good business. Five or six tables seating a mix of singles and couples were having dinner, and I sat at a table in the far end of the room hoping the other diners would shield me from Stretch's view. *Damn it. What kind of detective am I? Stretch knows what I look like; this was a dumb idea.* But I was committed. Stretch would be arriving any moment and he might see me if I picked up and left the building. I hoped he wouldn't stay long enough to ID me, or to stay for dinner.

A big breasted over the hill, beached blond, food server showed up after several minutes. She was curt, unsmiling, and unfriendly. *If you don't like your job why not quit and find another, bitch.* But I didn't voice my displeasure; I just ordered a hamburger and a Heineken and kept my big mouth shut. Maybe I should have ordered a Bud. It's not a good idea being conspicuous; this was not a Heineken crowd. The service was fast and within minutes I had the order unceremoniously dropped in front of me. The waitress forgot, or intentionally neglected to bring me ketchup for the burger, and I had to get it from the service pantry. I probably looked like an old codger who would only have one drink and leave a lousy tip. I'm sure the waitress wanted to see me out of the restaurant so she could fill the table with a younger couple. Young guys know how to put away the booze, run up a huge beverage tab, and leave a tip proportional to the bill.

I proceeded to eat my burger very slowly and tried to keep my face hidden in the beer while still having a view to the bar, and I didn't have to wait very long. Stretch came in, sat down at the end of the bar closest to the door, and ordered a Budweiser. Within a few minutes one of the bikers came over and sat on a stool next to him. They chatted for a few minutes, and the biker reached into his leather jacket, took out some bills and exchanged it for a packet, an envelope. I didn't have to guess twice about what was in the envelope.

Stretch finished his beer, got up and left without ever looking into the dining area. Thank God. My cover was not blown. I enjoyed the rest of my meal and left the bar leaving a very small tip. I didn't want to ruin the waitresses' opinion of me. Screw her.

***

When I got home I paced the floor thinking about what to do with Stretch. I felt exhilarated, more alive than I had been for months. I had assumed he was a drug dealer and now there was the eyewitness proof I needed. It was nothing that could be taken to the police of course. Even if I did they would not have done anything about it. Drug users were rampant everywhere in St. Petersburg as it is in all big cities.

If they locked up every small time junkie and dealer they would have to build so many jails it would bankrupt the state. No, this was a problem that would give me great pleasure in resolving, and it would save the taxpayers a lot of expense in the long run.

***

Killing Stretch outright was a solution, but not a good one. A quick end to his life would not net the source of his drugs, the people who supply him. He could easily be replaced. His job was a coveted one. Lots of guys would jump at the chance to make that kind of easy money. Getting rid of Stretch would only eliminate a small cog in a big machine. I had to think on a larger scale, to think big or stay at home. What was needed was to get to the local dealers source of supply, not the Columbian cartel perhaps, but to the next higher level of distribution above Stretch, the people who supply pushers. This would be my job. This is the drug traffic level the law often neglects. The local police usually don't bother with insignificant local distributors and pushers because if a small time user or dealer should happen to get caught he lawyers up and interrogation gets the cops nothing. But the police can't interrogate a suspect like I could, and there isn't any constitutional fifth amendment in my court of law.

***

Over the next two weeks I tailed Stretch, and rented different cars so as not to be recognized. I followed him each night starting from the last location he met with his dealers. This way I never had to follow him too long, nor too far, and being detected was minimized. He had eight stops, and his route never varied. Unfortunately I never saw him pick up his supply of drugs. I figured he must restock his stash on a Saturday or Sunday. But tailing him then was too dangerous as the traffic was very light on the weekend. I'll have to find a way to have him give up his source during one of his weekday runs.

Stretch never made a delivery on a Monday so I chose that day to drive the route he took, to duplicate the same time of night and the local road conditions, stopping at each stop he made, then getting out of my car and reconnoitering the area by walking up and down the streets where he made deliveries. I circled each adjoining block by foot, both North and South, and East and West, to see if there were any potential dangers that might complicate my mission. All I needed was to pick an interception spot with a police station around the corner and have a patrol car return to their home base while I was there. That could cause a problem or two, and I have enough problems. A few of the locations were immediately eliminated. One was on the corner of a street that had a playground with a basketball court with night illumination. Could you imagine an older white man lurking around an area full of six foot black teenagers on the way to the playground? I would probably get mugged for the change in my pocket so they could buy a beer after their game. Another location was near an all night convenience store. That certainly was out, too much foot traffic. But the fourth stop was just a street corner in the middle of nowhere, in an industrial area without any stores or pedestrians walking the street, and Stretch didn't get there until about 10:00 PM. The entire area was dark and lonely, a perfect place to intercept him.

My plan is to somehow get Stretch to leave his car before he met with his dealer. I certainly could not get to him while he was doing business with his contact. Then there would be two people to deal with and that was too risky. No, it would have to be in the industrial area, but before he made a delivery. I don't have the final plan figured out but I'm sure it will come to me. Meanwhile I could work out the other details, like getting a disguise and getting the tools and things needed to get a complete confession out of Stretch before killing him.

***

This morning I left the apartment early and ate a hardy breakfast of bacon and eggs at our local diner. And since this was a special day, and since I was in no rush I ordered a melon for an appetizer and a bagel instead of toast with the meal. Big spender from the East, but what the hell, this was a special day. The meal was a great treat, the waitress friendly and the atmosphere just right so I left the diner feeling great at a few minutes after 9:00 AM figuring that would be a good time to leave the city and miss the rush hour.

The local approaches to the highway were free of traffic and within a few minutes I was headed towards Orlando on the I-4. "So far so good", I thought. I hate road congestion and have enough pent up emotion without adding to it by getting stuck in stop and go traffic. I can understand road rage as I am often the one who precipitates an incident. But in Florida, where anyone can carry a lethal weapon, a gun, road rage is something a person wants to avoid.

***

The trip to Orlando took about two hours. I had previously searched the internet for the location of the stops I had planned to make so there was no need to waste time going store to store to find the goodies that were needed. My first stop was to a costume shop on Mills Avenue. They specialized in theatrical supplies, makeup, and the stuff Disney World might purchase. They carried everything I wanted, and a lot of things I didn't need, like transgender costumes. The new "me" was homophobic and if there was one thing I couldn't stand anymore it was being around a lot of queers. I parked my car on the street at a meter. *For Christ sake, I'm spending money here and they don't have free parking. Hell, I'm not feeding a lousy meter*. But then I thought better of it so I reluctantly inserted a quarter in the slot and entered the store, pissed off and ready for a fight.

An obviously gay salesman approached me. He got a little too close, right into my face, and I didn't like that one bit.

"Anything I can help you with sir?" he asked

"I'm looking for a wig and moustache for a costume party"

He flipped an imaginary cigar ash and said,

"Want to add Groucho Marx eyeglass, moustache, and big nose"

Just keep your distance Queenie or you'll be wearing a broken nose.

"Did you ever hear this funny quote of his?

I didn't answer but the told me anyway.

"A man is only as old as the woman he feels."

"Ha, yeah that's funny, but I think I'll just stay with the toupee and mustache. I'm going to a party as Tom Selleck, and as I recall Groucho didn't have much hair"

The salesman got serious. He finally picked up on my unfriendly vibes, cut the conversation short, and retrieved the merchandise from the stockroom. After trying out the wig for a proper fit he rang up the sale. The costume was very flattering, took a lot of years off my face, and sort of made me look a little like Tom Selleck. That thought made me feel a little better.

The second stop was to a gun shop that carried security items. A big guy approached me. *Jesus Christ, this guy must moonlight as a wrestler.*

"Can I get you something?" he growled. He wasn't angry; I think he was just practicing his wrestler voice.

"Yeah, I want to get my wife a weapon. Her sister got mugged while she was entering her house and now my wife is afraid to go out at night, so she wants some protection."

"Oh, that's too bad. Where did this happen?"

"Why do you want to know, are you going to burglar the neighborhood?" Quick thinking on my part; I haven't the foggiest idea as to neighborhoods in Orlando.

"Hey don't get excited."

"Sorry, it's just a sensitive subject. The bastard had a pair of tin snips and cut her sisters finger off to get the diamond ring, lots of blood, quite a mess."

"Oh, I'm sorry about that. These guys are getting very brazen and desperate for drug money. They would kill their mother if they had to for a fix."

"Well maybe I'll get the chance to save a mom."

I told the salesman I wanted something that shoots a dart, or a barb. It's the type of weapon that has a wire tethered to the gun so I wouldn't have to come into direct contact with a mugger when I zapped him. The salesman told me what I was referring to was a taser, and a retailer cannot sell a weapon like that to a walk in customer since it shoots a projectile. It's considered an offensive weapon, and

Florida law requires registration of this type of device. But he could sell a stun gun to a buyer off the street.

I couldn't use a credit card or give out any personal information that could connect me to a weapon so I had to settle for a direct contact stun gun. Direct contact was something that had to be avoided if possible but I had no choice and made an instant decision to go for it. I would have to catch my prey off guard to have any hope of surviving the encounter. A tussle with Stretch could go wrong with me possibly getting the stun gun shoved up my butt.

The third stop was to a patio shop. An ad on their website featured durable indoor-outdoor carpet, the type with nylon fibers, and a very low nap. It was the kind of carpet that withstood rain and can be washed without losing its color or texture. My plans for Stretch might result in a little blood and I had to be sure I could clean the carpet before I discarded it. I purchased the smallest rug they had, a 5x7 foot carpet. No sense in wasting money.

The last stop was to a Salvation Army vintage clothing store. I purchased a dark gray business suit and a pair of black wing tip shoes that went out of style when prohibition ended. The suit was a little threadbare, and wasn't the best fit. The shoes were a little tight, but I wasn't going to a job interview or going to be the best man at a wedding, and I hadn't planned on wearing it more than once.

By now it was approximately 4:30 PM. *Oh hell, I'm going to get stuck in rush hour traffic if I leave for St. Petersburg now.* So I stopped at an Applebee's and ordered a martini for an appetizer and a barbeque rib dinner. It was a welcome break to enjoy a stiff drink and a good dinner and to muse over the progress that was made. I felt great, excited, like a pit bull unchained and racing towards a helpless poodle. I thought about all the things I had bought and how to use them.

The remaining few items that I needed could be purchased locally, and never traced back to me. Things were going well. This was going to be fun, another perfect murder.

It was almost 6:00 PM when I finished dinner and entered the highway, route 4-W. The traffic was still fairly heavy, bumper-to-bumper in the Orlando area. At one point, while still in heavy traffic, I failed to stop in time, and hit a truck in the rear. The driver and I pulled over to the shoulder and exited our respective vehicles to examine the expected damage. I controlled my rising temper for a change. This accident was clearly my fault, and besides the driver of the truck was a giant. I wasn't going to get into it with him. He could have beaten me to a pulp with one hand tied behind his back.

When we examined the vehicles it was evident that there wasn't any damage. His truck had heavy solid steel bumpers and my van was a Nissan SUV with Buffalo bumpers. Buffalo bumpers are heavy tubular steel decorative bumpers that are in front of the car's original equipment, and they can take a good bang without denting. You see them on a lot of Land Rovers. Like someone is really going into the Serengeti, and might run into an elephant. Give me a break. But they do look cool. They were on the car when I purchased it, and they protected my car in this otherwise fender-bender.

I expressed my apologies to the truck driver for hitting him, and when he saw there was no damage he growled his acceptance for my contrition, got into his truck and drove away. As I continued the journey back to St. Petersburg I replayed the accident scene through my head. Eureka! I had an answer to a problem that had been plaguing me.

My problem was how to get Stretch to stop and get out of his car so I could zap him. I had earlier rejected the thought of just killing him with the shotgun. A simple drive by kill would have been easy and possibly not investigated by the police. When they saw the stash in Stretch's pocket they would assume the killing was just drug related. They would ignore the whole thing, just one less junkie off the street. More than likely if the police caught me at the scene of the crime all but the most gung- ho of them might thank me for the public service and let me go.

Blowing Stretch's head off was not an option. A simple killing would not get me to the next level up the drug distribution ladder. I would eventually get rid of Stretch. That would be the fun part, and I did deserve some fun for all the work and expense I was going through, but not before getting the information I was after. So it had to be a zapping with the stun gun however dangerous the operation might be. And before Stretch recovered from the shock I would have to immobilize and transport him to a secure location where I could interrogate him at my leisure, and then end his miserable, worthless life.

The eureka moment I had while driving home was the solution to the problem of getting to Stretch without me getting hurt or worse yet, dead. I would confront him during the route he took while delivering drugs to his customers. The scenario hopefully would go like this; I would intercept Stretch at a deserted location, on a street that he normally traveled, probably after his second delivery. He had to drive through an industrial area for his third drop, and there would be very few cars on the street at that time of night, virtually no traffic, and no retail stores. It was the most deserted area I could hope for. I would park on the street and wait for him to pass me. As he passed I would pull out of a parking slot and bump him with my vehicle. He would have to stop and get out of his car to examine the damage. More than likely his car will have a nasty dent in the passenger side of the car while I should not have any damage thanks to the Buffalo bumpers. I would then get out of my van and apologize for my careless driving, and for not looking behind me when I pulled the car out of the parking spot. I can be very fawning when I have to be. I'm a pretty good actor and played the Marlon

Brando part in *A Streetcar Named Desire* back in high school, and if I say so myself, I did a hell of a job.

If all went well, Stretch would not recognize me. The wig and the black moustache would hide my facial features, and wearing a suit should definitely disarm him. I would look like a businessman who may have been working late, perhaps exiting from an empty office building behind the car. He would have no suspicion of what was about to happen. The business suit jacket would reinforce my innocuous appearance, but more importantly the inside pocket of the jacket would hide the stun gun effectively. He on the other hand would be in a short sleeve shirt and his bare arm would be an easy target for the immobilizing shock.

We will have to exchange insurance cards, and when he either reached into the glove box of his car, or reached for his wallet, I would zap him on his arm. I expect from what the gun salesman told me he would fall to the ground and writhe in an uncontrollable seizure, like a freshly caught fish flopping about the deck of a fishing skiff. He would not even be able to scream or cry for help, and while he was helpless I would bind his wrists, gag him, toss him into the SUV, and drive away to an area where I could interrogate him at my leisure. If something went wrong and Stretch did recognize me I would reach into the car, retrieve the shotgun, and blow him to pieces. But I don't want to think about that. I have enough to worry about.

The rest of the trip back to St. Petersburg was uneventful. The traffic eased up and my temper cooled down. Thankfully I got home safely, all in one piece. When I arrived back at the apartment there was no one on the complex grounds or on the patio chomping at the bit for the opportunity to ask where I was all day. Actually no one ever asked what I had done during the day. We all mind our own business. For all I knew I could be living among a gaggle of mass murderers and not have a clue about their nefarious activities. Nobody asks and nobody tells. That's what I liked about my new home.

***

After the trip to Orlando, and for the next few days, I slept like a newborn baby, waking up each morning well rested and with a clear mind. I felt a lot happier knowing there was a viable plan for ending Stretch's career, and with nothing else to think about I figured it was about time to make some friends. I had not met, or socialized with anyone since moving to St. Petersburg, I didn't need to, all my thoughts were initially focused on my internal anger and then with the mission. However, while I wanted to make a few friends, getting involved with some of the guys living in the apartment complex was off the table. It's not a good idea to mix business with pleasure. All the tenants keep to themselves, and it would be better to keep it that way. So I figured the best way to meet people outside of my immediate neighborhood was to hang around a tennis court. And besides, I thought it might be a good time to start playing tennis again after such a very long hiatus. I had not played the game since leaving New York, and my waistline was beginning to indicate the lack of exercise. A few laps in the pool every day just wasn't enough to keep the extra pounds off.

The next morning was the day I would begin the transition from being a loner to what I hoped was a normal person with a few friends. I skipped breakfast so I would be able to move about the court without feeling bloated, had a cup of coffee, filled a mug with another cup, packed a buttered bagel, and left for the local recreation area, the one with tennis courts. While driving to the park my thoughts wandered to how my outlook on life had improved now that there was something to occupy my mind. During the past few months I had frequent periods of depression, and now I was beginning to feel better about myself. Was I entering into a manic state? I think my problem might be that I am a bit mentally ill. Maybe I'm bipolar. No, that couldn't be right. I never had this condition before I used the Ouija board. Is it possible that all bipolar sufferers have two entities inside them, each one in turn making its presence felt? It would explain a lot. It would explain why I went from a peaceful good natured person into Mr. Hyde overnight.

We are hearing more instances of people going postal, shooting up personnel in the office they work in or at schools they attend, all for no good reason. They want revenge for some real or perceived grievance, and take it out in blood.

You read about bizarre instances of men and women thinking they are werewolves, baying at a full moon, and often getting quite violent, capable of inhuman vicious acts. We are hearing of people who are obsessed with drinking blood because they think themselves vampires. Wicca's think they are witches and warlocks. Off the wall religious groups such as the snake worshippers caress and cover their body with rattlesnakes and other venomous creatures. If that's not crazy, what is?

Maybe all of the psychos in institutions and those walking the streets are not really psychotic at all, but simply have an evil ethereal spirit sharing their body. It could explain why there are so many nut cases walking the streets today. Mental illnesses are not fully understood. No one really knows why we do the things we do. Psychology is still in its infancy. All psychologists know is how to mask symptoms with heavy drugs. I know a few shrinks who are crazier than I am, although in a different way. How are they going to help? It's like the blind leading the blind.

***

When I arrived at the park there was a foursome on the court playing doubles, and outside the court on the sidelines two men my age were hanging out waiting for some players to show up so they could get a game going. They could have played singles if they were twenty years younger, but like me they were in no condition to play a fast game.

Two men were sitting on a bench at a concrete checkers table adjacent to the tennis court. I walked over and introduced myself.

"Hi Guys, looking for game?"

They looked apprehensive, and I couldn't blame them. This is a touchy subject. After all, they didn't know what level I played at, and nobody wants a rank amateur in their game. But being a gentleman one of them said,

"Yeah, but we still need a fourth, and I don't think anyone else will show up today. If you want to play Canadian, and take the singles slot I'll have a go at it."

I thought about the offer for a moment but decided that it was not a good idea. A couple of years earlier I wound up in the hospital after playing a singles match. I was sure I had a heart attack on the court. It was on a hot summer day and we were playing at one of my friend's private club in a non air-conditioned court. It must have been well over 100 degrees in the building. I was sweating profusely and losing salt and potassium. Suddenly I had a severe pain in my left arm, and was overcome with vertigo and dizziness, and a moment later collapsed on the court. My buddy called 911 and an ambulance was dispatched in minutes. The EMS came to my rescue and rushed me to the local hospital where they took all sorts of tests, kept me bed for two days, and finally sent me home after determining that I only had a case of heat exhaustion coupled with dehydration. This experience indicated two things. Hospitals have to play the defensive medicine game and Medicare must pay hospitals a great deal for presumed heart attacks.

"No thanks, I don't have the legs for it" I replied, "I'm strictly a doubles player."

"Me too, singles are for the kids. I haven't seen you here before. Did you just move into town?"

He's getting nosey already. Maybe making friends is not such a good idea.

"Yes, I'm from New York but the winters are getting to be too much for this old body and with my wife gone there was nothing to keep me up north. Besides I have some family living in Dade County, far enough away so I don't have to see them all the time, but close enough to spend holidays with."

They laughed at that comment and the ice was broken. We bantered about for a bit. I put on my friendliest face, didn't curse, and in general was a very amiable guy. First impressions count when you're trying to make new friends. Funny thing, I wasn't acting. I really wanted to make a friend or two. This must be my manic state.

I changed the subject and said,

"I see there are a quite a few checker tables here. Does anyone use them for chess?"

"Yeah, if you come by after 1:00 PM there will be a few players looking for a game."

"Great, maybe I'll do that."

We chatted for a while longer and made plans to meet the next day only earlier in the hope that more players might be on hand. After a few more minutes it looked like my new friends were getting restless and wanting to find an excuse to leave. Bob broke the ice; he looked at his watch and announced:

"Hey guys, I have to get home and get something to eat before my blood sugar drops. This diabetes is a pain in the ass. It controls my life."

Ray broke in,

"And I have to get home to make lunch for Ruth. Her condition is getting worse; she hardly ever gets out of bed now".

I didn't say anything but I thought it's hell to get old.

And so we all went our separate ways. There was no rush for me to get home so I toured the park. It was a beautiful well-kept facility. Aside from the recreational sports areas there was a large cluster of pines and deciduous trees with the remaining areas devoted to grass. Five tennis and two handball courts were located at one end, and in the far corner, a night lighted ball field. The school kids probably played little league baseball on Saturdays, and the men probably played softball on Sundays. I walked to the wooded area, sat down under the shade of a black walnut tree to eat my bagel, and finish the now cold coffee.

A half hour later I brushed the crumbs off my lap and went home, changed into a swimsuit, took a dip, and lounged at the pool. Ah, this was the life. It's like being on vacation. When I had been sufficiently broiled by the midday sun I left the pool area and went back to the apartment for a late lunch. I chose one of my favorite meals, two nuked burritos and a beer. I've been trying to cut down on my caloric intake and a beef burrito is my idea of a low fat diet. And let's not forget the beer; it was a Bud light even though I would rather have had Guinness Stout. A heavy Irish brew, now that is what I call a beer.

After lunch it was naptime. It's something one should not do after eating a meal. That's no way to lose a few pounds. But I like to take a nap so what the hell, I'll try and have a light dinner, maybe a frozen Hungry Man meal. There's nothing better than a good greasy fried chicken dinner, and it goes great with beer.

I usually fall asleep almost immediately on a full stomach, but sleep eluded me. I kept reviewing the dichotomy of my mind, how I could be a nice person one moment and a ruthless killer the next. My mind would just not let go of it.

Why am I suddenly so full of contradictions? How could I suddenly be happy when I was so agitated a few days ago? Once again I made the case for being bipolar, manic one day and depressed the next. I'm short-tempered and often angry for no reason at all. That is something I never was before the "cure". I'm different that's for sure, but not bipolar. I don't have all the required symptoms. My ups and downs can be minutes apart. A true manic–depressive has mood swings lasting for weeks at a time. Perhaps I'm schizophrenic. However, I think not as there are no voices in my head telling me what to do. I'm not delusional either, and don't exhibit other symptoms typical of a schizophrenic. I couldn't have a multiple personality disorder either because a person with that condition has two or more very distinct personalities separate from each other. When one is at the forefront he doesn't know the other exists. On the other hand, I (for all the good it does me) am fully aware which personality is in control.

August 2nd

I awoke early as usual, looked out the window and saw that it had rained during the night. The sky was overcast and it threatened to be a miserable day. Tennis would be out. It didn't make sense going to the park at such an early hour, as my new friends probably would not be there. I thought if it cleared up I might go out after lunch, and see if there were a few chess players looking to sharpen their skills on a newbie.

I hadn't played chess since college, but with all the free time on my hands it might be a good time to get back in the game. The more experienced players would make mincemeat of me, but that's all right. I wouldn't get angry because I expect to be beaten. I only get angry when someone cheats, does me wrong, or gets on my nerves. And that's normal, or at least for me it's normal. What's not normal though is thinking it's okay to kill someone to right a wrong. That's my little not so normal quirk.

It turned out to be a wet, rainy day. When it wasn't raining cats and dogs the sky remained overcast and foreboding. There is nothing worse than a rainy day in Florida and I get bored with nothing to do. In fact I get bored very quickly now. I never used to. I used to look forward to a rainy day so I could curl up in an easy chair and read a good novel. Now I hardly ever read anything except the newspaper and an occasional novel if it's an easy read. There was nothing on the TV except afternoon soap operas and I would sooner poke myself in the eye with a sharp stick than watch the trials and tribulations of a TV housewife. The plots are so simple a five year old could write them. Day after day the programs chronicle men and woman cheating on their respective spouses or lovers. A variation of the story line might include a cheating wife who has an incurable disease. Having a disease is bad enough, but her lover has left for a younger girl. The wife will suffer and bravely linger on (but won't die if they find a last minute cure) until the season comes to an end. And the plot may thicken. She may also have a husband who has just lost his job, and a handicapped child who is bullied at school. Did I forget anything?

So having nothing to do, I left the apartment after lunch and went to the mall. You get to watch an army of old retirees walking the mall for exercise with no intention of stopping at a store to buy something or of parting with any of the little SSI check they receive each month. But I had a purpose for being at the mall and it wasn't for a stroll down the wide boulevards. I decided to get a roommate, someone to talk to. Someone I can reveal all my innermost secret thoughts to, and someone who won't judge me, or answer back. I went to a pet store and bought a kitten, a cute little guy with a gray coat and white paws.

***

Ever since I could remember I had a pet, and I can clearly remember the first one. I was about seven years old and wanted something to care for, so I pestered my parents until they finally got tired of my whining and bought into our home a pet which would not interfere with their life. They bought me a turtle. The little fellow lasted for a few months before dying of unknown causes, and several weeks passed before I worked up the courage to approach my parents on the subject of a replacement pet. For some reason I could not reconcile the turtle's death with my culpability. I thought I did something wrong and it was my fault the turtle died. What I did not realize at the time was that you can't paint a turtle to make it look more appealing, but that's what sellers of little critters did in those days. They dyed the little chicks yellow for Easter and little turtles blue or red or whatever color they though might sell. However the death of the blue colored turtle made me even more introverted than I already was, and it showed up in my relationship with people and in my school grades.

Looking back I think I was also a neglected child, and that is what may have contributed to my quirky personality. Not that I was abused, mind you, but my brother Steven was always the shining star in our family when we were young children, the apple of my parent's eye. Many years later when I proved my worth both Steven and I both enjoyed the love and affectation of our parents. We were one happy family. But during my formative years Steven was the bright one with the good marks in school. In a Jewish family good grades and a superior intelligence were the most important attributes. It meant everything.

My brother was earmarked for college at an early age, and after seeing my grammar school grades my father wanted to send me to a trade school instead of a high school where I could at least get an academic diploma. Fortunately my mom prevailed. No son of hers was ever going to be a tradesman. And so I went to Flushing High and managed to graduate with a regent's diploma and marks high enough for college. I guess it might be said that I was a late bloomer because I did not get a degree until I was twenty-six, after a four year enlistment in the Air Force, and on the G.I. bill. My brother Steven on the other hand made it into Princeton on a scholarship right out of high school.

When I finally accepted the fact that the death of the turtle was not my fault, and that a real animal might survive unless I really screwed up, I pestered my folks for another pet, and not another reptile. I moped around the house and carried on until my mother finally gave in and got me a kitten from the local animal shelter. What I really wanted was a dog but that was asking for too much as we lived in an apartment, and my dad was not going down five floors to walk a mutt even though the building had an elevator. I can't say my dad hated animals but he sure didn't want any as pets.

The kitten was a Christmas present, and I think it was the only present I received that year. Money was short and a free pet from the animal shelter made more sense than a toy purchased at a department store. The kitten was about six weeks old and at the age when everything was an object to be played with, scratched, or torn to shreds. Unfortunately, after exploring our apartment for a day or two the little rascal found my moms single pair of dress stockings and rendered them into little scraps of silk. This was during the war long before inexpensive nylon's were available, and silk stockings were a treasure almost impossible to obtain. My mother seldom got angry, but this time she went through the roof, and the cat was gone the next day.

***

After leaving the mall I stopped at the local supermarket, left my new little pet in the car and picked up a litter box for the kitten, and dinner for us both. I kept the shopping to a minimum as I was fearful the kitten might begin to cry and alert a nosey passerby who would call the authorities to report me for animal abuse. Wouldn't that be ironic, my true identity being revealed because of a cat? I was losing focus. I swore my life would be that of a loner, and now I was sharing it with a friend, albeit only a pet.

The first thing I did when I got home was to fix dinner. I bought the most expensive cat food for the little guy, and for myself – a not so expensive frozen pizza. Hey, you have to watch the budget with two mouths to feed. The cat, still unnamed, ate like he had not eaten a meal since being weaned from his mother. I picked at the pizza. It was awful, like eating tomato paste covered cardboard. *Screw the budget, next time I'll order pizza from a pizzeria.*

Afterwards, when he and I finished our respective meals, I settled into the recliner to watch a TV show and tuned in the military channel. The Battle for the Pacific (in brilliant living color) was on, and Okinawa was up in flames.

The kitten jumped up onto my lap, curled into a furry ball, and immediately fell asleep. I stared at the TV screen with unfocused eyes, deep in random disjointed thoughts, and all of the thoughts were bits and snips of who we are, what makes us tick, and why.

Bombs dropped on the beachhead, and warships were obscured in clouds of smoke as the navy ships fired round after round of artillery shells into the Japanese troops defending their Pacific island. But little of the mayhem registered on my unfocused brain. All I saw on the TV was violence; the story line escaped me. I sat in the easy chair staring into the screen and it made no more sense to me than it would have made to the kitten. Images of slaughter, carnage, and torn bodies flashed before my eyes. Scenes of flamethrowers turning men into funeral pyres filled the screen. Eventually I became aware of what I was watching and it disturbed me. I who enjoy the thrill of killing wondered why there is an entire TV network devoted to the art of war. Is it possible that millions of men are just like me? Is it in man's nature to want to destroy instead of creating and building for the betterment of mankind? Is it possible the audience lives vicariously through the solder's eye, wishing they could be the one to kill and maim.

If the show had some redeeming value instead of just showing senseless slaughter and gratuitous brutality it might have had some justification, but there was none. The thinly veiled documentary was just an excuse to feed man's violent nature.

****

After watching the brutal TV show I thought about man's inhumanity, his brutality and cruelty, his intolerance and indifference to the suffering of his fellow man, and became convinced foreign entities might reside in more human bodies than we ever suspected. Although difficult to accept, rogue spirits might be the ones responsible for a great deal of the insanity we witness. But that does not mean all the evil in the world can be traced to evil spirits. After all, it only takes one Hitler to set in action a course of events resulting in 50 million deaths. The soldiers wielding the flamethrowers and the flight crews of aircraft who drop bombs on innocent civilians were doing so because they believed their country's because was justified and necessary. It only takes a few men to start a war. Unfortunately the innocent have to finish it.

To keep things in perspective you have to look at the big picture. I don't think possession by entities from another dimension can account for all of the madness in the world. It might be man's nature to have a violent gene or two buried deep within his chromosomes. The genes were formed eons ago, back to a time when it was necessary for survival, to kill or be killed. I remember back in the 1970's parents tried to nurture the softer side of their male children by forbidding them to play with toy guns and G.I. Joe dolls. But it didn't work. The child would pick up a broomstick and make believe it was a gun, and played war games with his friends. If you gave a male child a doll with a pink dress he would probably use it for target practice, or play werewolf and rip the doll's head off. It's going to take more than a few years to lose the errant gene and evolve into a peaceful human being.

But we are making progress. When you consider that the Cro-Magnon man, the first truly modern Homo sapien, has been around for at least 40,000 to 60,000 years you can see it's going to take a while to evolve and lose some of our more violent genes. As recently as two thousand years ago Romans thought it was great sport for Gladiators to kill each other, and for slave owners to dispose of their property like a piece of garbage if they so desired. And let's not forget the Crusaders. They slaughtered innocent men, women and children by the thousands. But to moderate my viewpoint I suppose some of the Crusaders thought they were doing God's work, and it's possible the average foot soldier was following orders as did the German Wehrmacht recruit who shot innocent people because his superior officer told him to.

So that brings us up to today. I don't think the average person thinks it is perfectly normal or even acceptable to kill another human being over a trivial matter. He may want to let his errant malevolent gene take control of his body, but his soul, his inner being prevents him from doing so. The soul is eternal. It incarnates from one life to another, and it behooves the inner spirit to live virtuously and not commit evil deeds, as the entity will never achieve the peaceful state of Nirvana with a soiled soul.

While I admit my opinions are non-empirical and speculative in nature half the world's population concurs with many of my beliefs. Hindus and Buddhists alike believe in an afterlife, in reincarnation. Their dogma differs slightly from each other, however both religions believe a soul will return in a living form, to reincarnate. Life is eternal in one form or another, and will repeat itself until the spirit attains its ultimate goal of Nirvana, the serene place where the Astral body will spend eternity.

Another basic Buddhist and Hindu belief is Karma. Most of us mistakenly confuse karma with fate, but it's altogether different. Fate refers to forces outside of your control that make things happen. An example would be if you miss your bus and while you are waiting for another one you meet a person who you will become your spouse. Karma is a force generated by a person's actions in his current life to perpetuate transmigration and its consequences to determine the person's next existence.

There is good Karma and bad. It is the consequence of our actions here on earth. In effect what you do in this life will determine your fate in the next. "As you sow, so shall you reap" may explain the pain and suffering we experience here on earth.

Perhaps those we perceive to be helpless victims, people that are raped or murdered for the spare change in their pocket, or those who die in landslides and volcanoes, or are victims of ethnic cleansing are reaping their reward for the evil they perpetrated in a past life. It doesn't seem fair, but Karma explains it all.

However there are also other considerations aside from retribution for evil deeds done in past incarnations that may explain pain and misery. The ethereal spirit inside our body has lived many lives. In its present incarnation an entity may choose the life of a blind mute, or a victim of a crime, someone who dies at an early age short of what we think of as a normal lifespan just to experience the suffering, or to add a few chits to the Nirvana Savings Bank. A life of suffering for the Astral body equates to a zealot's flagellation of his body with a cat-o-nine tails. It seems absurd to most of us, but peeling the skin from one's back is an act of devotion designed to bring the person's soul closer to his God by suffering His pain. Who are we to judge another's beliefs, and his highway to heaven?

War, famine, natural disasters, pain and suffering, all of the misery we experience here on Earth has been written in the book of life, the Akashic records. However it is the individual spirit that determines his place in the grand scheme of things. An Astral body must make a choice and decide on the life he wants to live. If an entity seeks redemption for past sins he may choose a human body that is destined to live a life of suffering and pain. We all make our own choice even though the natural evolution of our world and the entire universe is pre-determined.

Consider the four seasons, winter followed by spring, then into summer and fall. Each season has its time and place. It has been this way in the past and it will be this way in the future. The seasons are eternal. However, we the individual, may choose to dress warmly in the cold. We don't have to. Nobody forces us to protect our body from frostbite. If we wanted to die we could freeze to death. It's our choice, and our personal decisions do not affect the progression of the seasons.

Pain and suffering, redemption and purification are part of an endless cycle repeated over and over again into the infinite dimension of time and space. And it will continue until it ends with the ultimate goal of Nirvana. Then and only then will a soul, the timeless entity that is us, become one with the universal spirit, the one we call God.

Why then, if a soul is incarnated with an objective, a noble purpose, does it at times change personalities in the midstream of his life? If an entity comes back to our world and chooses to live a virtuous life so it may eventually achieve the state of Nirvana why would it suddenly become evil for no good reason? Why are some people born normal, a good and loving son or daughter, an honor student in school, a pillar in his community, and then suddenly turn bad, shooting up his workplace, and killing dozens of his co-workers? Did the Astral body change his mind? Did the soul suddenly decide that it's more fun to take the easy way out, and to rob a bank instead of working for a living? I don't think so. The soul has too many past incarnations under its belt to do something so stupid; to set back the goal of attaining the state of Nirvana, and having to start all over again.

If for many years a person has lived an exemplary life, and is happy, and his life bountiful, it is because the entity wants to live a productive life in his or her current incarnation. But if suddenly a human body is invaded and possessed by another spirit, an evil one, the result will be a tormented soul, a person deemed to be mentally disturbed, capable of violent acts and anti-social behavior.

Possession by an entity, either evil or benign, is rarely seen or discussed but it is more common than one might think. We are embarrassed to talk about first hand knowledge of the paranormal. It's like admitting you believe in flying saucers, and as the sophisticated skeptic knows, only fruitcakes believe in aliens from outer space. However in spite of the intellectuals and the many psychiatrists who deny even the possibility of a supernatural universe, hundreds of exorcisms are performed every year in this country and throughout the world. But the rituals are often hushed up and seldom publicized.

It seems to me that many organized religions often consider an exorcism an embarrassment to be kept in the closet while they should instead rejoice in banishing a demon and saving a soul. You don't always have to die to be saved.

Demonic possession has been observed and recorded by every civilization throughout history and while I don't think there is a demon, something from hell inside me, I think this is what happened: I intentionally allowed another entity into my physical body, and the entity cured my malignant tumor.

Spontaneous remissions and miraculous cures are nothing new. It happens all the time. We call it a misdiagnosis on the doctors' part, or a miracle, and attribute the miracle to God. More likely our ethereal spirit, may if it so chooses, direct our body to activate yet undiscovered curative elements which circulate through our bloodstream. And these elements once energized isolate and destroy that which may harm us. This is what I think happened in my body. I think this is why I was cured. But there were ramifications I had never anticipated.

***

Up to the time of the cancer scare I was a normal human being, happy, cheerful, loving, and good-natured. But my personality changed immediately after the Ouija session. I morphed into a completely different person. I was until a few days ago, angry, belligerent, and consumed with hate. I even began to loathe the wife I once loved. However things have changed. In the last several days I have begun to experience emotions I thought were lost forever. I'm still different, but not as much as before. Therefore it is my belief that my original Astral body was never displaced and there are two entities inside my body, and they have learned to live with each other, to compromise, and share my physical shell. I don't hate or feel anger with the same passion as before, although I still have the uncontrollable compulsion to kill.

So now my problem is, how do I get rid of the second entity sharing space with my original soul so I can be a nice guy again, or on the other hand do I really want to get rid of the new spirit? Obviously the Astral body I was born with wanted to die, (for what reason I don't know. Perhaps his mission on Earth was filled) but the new one wants to live. I think I'll side with the new one. However the downside of having the new spirit sharing my body is that he has a compulsion to kill people. But perhaps I can channel the murderous urge to those who deserve it. I can be an avenging vigilante and rid the world of some evil people. I can live with that.

****

The next morning after a good night sleep I awoke bright eyed and bushy tailed. My mind was clear. The issue of my identity was resolved the night before, and I was ready to continue the pursuit of the task I had set out to accomplish, making the world a better place to live in by getting rid of Stretch and his cohorts.

After a light breakfast of toast and coffee I went to a Walmart on the other side of town and purchased the few remaining things I needed. The items were so common they could never be traced back to me. Everyone uses ducat tape; one roll more or less could never be identified, and the same goes for the plastic ties you use to secure a garbage bag.

After paying for the items I got into my car, buckled up and prepared to go to the next stop on my list. It was for another item that might prove useful. It was for something I thought of while relating the fictional story of my sister- in-law's mugging to the stun gun salesman, and how she lost her diamond ring. So I drove to the other end of the mall, entered the Home Depot and purchased a bolt cutter, the largest one they had. You can do a lot of things with a bolt cutter. It wasn't just for cutting bolts.

The shopping list competed, I entered an address I had found on the internet, and entered it into the Nissan's navigation system. The address was for a Catholic monastery and I drove to it in less than a half hour. When I arrived at the site it was as I had hoped for. It was at the edge of town where there are more orange groves than homes. The monastery was in a remote location and abandoned.

The sun was setting below the horizon when I pulled up to the front gate, and the grounds looked desolate and foreboding; perfect setting for a ghost movie, and I smiled to myself thinking that perhaps I will add a ghost who will walk the grounds for all eternity.

The Benedictine order of Saint Ignatius had suffered the fate of many religious facilities. There are not enough religious men, or women, in our hedonistic society willing to devote their lives to God and to live a monastic life of prayer and solitude to justify and maintain all the active retreats, so St. Ignatius was put on the chopping block. The complex had been purchased by a developer and earmarked to be demolished and to be replaced with a sub division of single-family homes. Unfortunately the housing bubble burst and if there was something Florida did not need it was more unsold homes. And so the project was shelved until the economy would recover. I wouldn't hold my breath. It's going to take twenty years for the housing sector to improve in this part of the country.

The compound consisted of several buildings on about six acres surrounded by a cyclone fence with an ornate wrought iron gate secured with a padlock. Good thing I bought a bolt cutter, although I didn't think I had to use it so soon when I made the purchase. I had other plans for the tool.

After carefully cutting the padlock in such a manner so that it could still be returned to the hasp on the gate, and appear to be locked, I let myself in. Then I drove about the grounds looking for signs of recent or present use. It was deserted as I had hoped. With the economy bad as it is there was always a chance squatters had moved in, but this was not the case. I had the place all to myself. After examining each building from the comfort of the van I choose the maintenance garage to be my workshop. It was isolated from the other buildings, far away from the street, and at the rear end of the compound. The location was perfect for my needs. An additional plus was that the monastery property ended a few yards behind the building, and there was another few hundred yards of meadow serving as a buffer from civilization. I drove to the garage and parked my vehicle under a small group of trees adjacent to the building. The van was well hidden.

The garage was a 40x40 foot one story cinder block building, the type of construction popular back in the 1960's. It had a single front door, one side window and a double overhead garage door facing the driveway. The front door was unlocked and I entered the dark cavernous open space. The electricity was turned off but fortunately I had a flashlight. The beam of light indicated that the room was empty except for a workbench, a few office chairs and metal shelving along one wall. Three cans of 30 weight motor oil and a few oil filters sat on the shelves. I'm a scavenger, and was hoping there might be some tools left behind or something of value that I could take home with me. No such luck.

Having done all I set out to do I left the grounds and replaced the useless padlock on the gate. The odds were small that someone would notice the missing section of the lock before I came back, and hopefully if all went as planned, I would be returning in a day or two for just one last visit.

***

The trip home was uneventful and I opened the door to see the little kitten mewing and demanding attention. It's nice to have a friend who loves and needs you. I kicked off my shoes, changed into more comfortable clothes, fixed a double martini to settle my nerves, and prepared dinner. The kitten feasted on the best cat food I could find, the Sheba brand. I don't know if it was the most nutritious brand, but it certainly was the most expensive. My dinner was a micro-waved frozen hamburger, and not the most expensive. Money had to be saved somewhere. After dinner I collapsed into the recliner and watched a little TV. Immediately after sitting down the kitten jumped up on my lap and I stroked his soft fur. The little guy looked up into my eyes and purred. He was happy and content, and so was I.

At 10:00 PM I turned on and tuned the television set to the weather channel. If conditions were right the next day would be the day of reckoning for Stretch, the culmination of all the plans, and the satisfaction of my murderous impulses, which, by the way, were not quite as murderous as they were a month or two earlier. But I hate to leave things undone. Once I start something it has to be finished. And besides, I had a lot of time and money invested in this venture, and I would be doing a worthwhile service for society by getting rid of a worthless parasite.

According to the weather channel conditions were predicated to be clear in the morning and changing to light rain beginning in the evening, and I was not sure if they boded well for what had to be done. I vacillated between two choices, going ahead with the plan, or rescheduling for better conditions. On the one hand if it rained the van might leave tire tracks, and my shoes might leave footprints in the mud, identifiable clues to the police. On the other hand if it remained clear there would be more cars and pedestrians on the streets thus maximizing the chances of being identified. I opted for the rain and turned my mind to other considerations. I thought about stealing a license plate from another vehicle and mounting it on my van, but I don't think anyone ever looks at a license plate, and the risk of being caught in the act of stealing a plate was too great. I would just have to risk using my own SUV and my own license plates and trust to fate.

***

The next morning I reviewed the plan to see if anything was overlooked, to see if all the bases were covered, and to my dismay I realized they were not.

How could I have been so stupid as to use my own vehicle? I don't think Stretch had seen my car, or knew what I drove, but he might have. I could not take that chance. I would have to rent a suitable vehicle, one that didn't dent easily.

After breakfast I drove to the local Land Rover dealership and rented the biggest SUV they had, the one with strong solid steel crash proof bumpers.

That evening I had a light dinner of frozen fish sticks with fries. A Hungry Man meal would have been too much, and might slow me down when I needed to be nimble. After dinner I fed the cat now named Kitty. I know the name "Kitty" is not very unique, but I never was good at naming pets, and since I always say, "Here Kitty- Kitty," when I call her it seemed like a logical handle.

I packed a laundry bag with the vintage suit, the shoes I had purchased at the Salvation Army store, and a white shirt and tie. Some dirty clothes, and the few necessities needed for the evening's work also went into the satchel. I thought the laundry bag was a brilliant idea as I didn't have a washer in the apartment and it would look like I was just going out to do some laundry. And in fact I would do my laundry when the deed was done. It was the perfect cover story. I then exited my apartment dressed in blue jeans, a short shirt to match, and sneakers, and drove off to the pre-determined location.

The traffic was light, probably more so because of the rain, and I drove the van a few blocks past the interception point to an area that was even more deserted. It was at an employee parking lot, behind an empty warehouse, another casualty of the recession. As expected it was void of cars, trucks, storage sheds or any signs of human habitation. After parking in the rear of the lot I changed into the businessmen's outfit, spread out the indoor-outdoor carpet so it covered the vehicle's rear interior, and set up the necessary accessories. The moustache and wig took only a few minutes to put on and when I looked in the mirror I liked what I saw, an old Tom Selleck. The stun gun went into the inside pocket of the suit jacket and it didn't create a bulge, a perfect disguise. Having satisfied myself that everything was ready I drove back to a parking spot in front of the empty building that had been selected and waited for Stretch to arrive.

In my old life I would have been scared out of my mind doing what I was about to do. Anticipation is the worst part; too much time to think of all the things that could go wrong. My first concern was that Stretch might recognize me even though the makeup looked good. Another worry was that my physical strength is no match for Stretch; he could very easily overpower me. If I didn't get a good zap the first time there would not be a second chance. He would make mince meat of me. Also, did I really think it was worth it to risk spending the rest of my life in jail if I get caught? And then I thought that even if I do not get caught after the deed is done who would get the blame in Akashicia, the old me, or the new one. Whose entity will have to pay for this murderous act, if indeed it is an evil act and not justice metered out for a person who deserved his fate? Will karma demand that I have to endure my worst fear in the next incarnation – to have to live as a blind beggar in Mumbai?

***

The time for thinking was past. Stretch's car appeared in the SUV's rear view mirror, and as it approached my car I pulled out of the parking spot like a bolt of lightning. The sound of crunching metal exploded in my ears as my bumper collided with his car's passenger door. I stopped, and we both got out of our cars. With a concerned and apologetic voice I said, "Hey buddy, I'm sorry but I didn't see you. There's never anyone coming down the street this time of night and I just didn't look. I'm so sorry. Can I make this right? I'll pay for the damage or we can turn it into the insurance company; whatever you say."

This completely disarmed Stretch. What was he going to do, beat up an old man? This wouldn't get his car fixed. Luckily Stretch spent most of the time looking at the dent and not at me. I said nervously, and I didn't have to put on an act, I was as scared as one can be, "Here is my driver's license and I.D."

And at the same time I reached into the jacket pocket, pulled out the stun gun, and zapped him on his bare forearm keeping the gun in contact with his body for at least three seconds. A stun duration of longer than three seconds might have killed him, and I certainly did not want him dead, at least not until the interrogation was completed.

Stun guns range in power from 200,000 volts to over a million. I wasn't cutting corners when I bought the gun. I got the biggest bad assed gun they had and the shock dropped Stretch to the ground like a sack of potatoes thrown from a second story window. He was instantly paralyzed, speechless, and writhing about the ground like a beached whale, and would remain so for several minutes. I quickly opened the rear hatch of my vehicle, removed the ducat tape, and bound his hands behind his back using the nylon ties, and ducat tape to back it up. I also put a 2-foot strip of tape across his mouth and completely around his head circling it two times. He wasn't going to yell, scream or say anything. I then blindfolded him and covered the cloth with tape. By this time stretch was beginning to recover from the debilitating shock, and was capable of movement. I said to him, "Don't worry I'm not going to kill you. That's why I blindfolded you, so you can't identify me. Just do as I say and you won't get hurt. Get into the van. It's going to be alright."

Stretch didn't say anything. He was still disorientated and couldn't utter a sound except for a soft moaning noise. But he did start to squirm and fuss until my assurance that he would not be killed quieted him down. He began to relax, and to accept the helpless position he was in. I led him to the rear door of the van and he quietly got in with my help. The rental vehicle had only two bench seats to allow for more cargo room so Stretch had to sit on the floor. I taped him to the rear of the back seat so he could not get up and alarm a pedestrian or passengers in another car. The only person who could possibly see Stretch would be a driver of a large truck with a passenger compartment high above the road. I had to remember not to pass any such vehicles. Stretch's seating arrangement was not what you might call comfortable, but it was the lap of luxury compared to what I had planned for him. I then put on rubber gloves; the inexpensive disposable ones that were purchased at the Home Depot paint department, and went through his car, and located a sports bag that I assumed contained drugs. Sure enough, inside the bag was a cache of sandwich bags with white powder. I opened a few bags, spilled most of the powder on the front seat, and took the rest of the dope with me. I had no use for the drugs but this had to look like a shake down robbery. When the cops arrived I wanted them to think this was some sort of drug deal gone wrong.

There was also a wad of cash in the sports bag and I intended to keep it. I could always use more cash. I then returned to my van, locked the door, took one last look at the bumper of my vehicle to make sure there were no scratches, and drove off to the next location, or should I say venue since the definition of the word also means "where justice is metered out".

Things were going well. There wasn't any damage to the rented SUV and the street was empty for the few minutes it took to apprehend Stretch. Even then, knowing the abduction was going as planned, my heart beat faster than a snared rabbit's looking up at a hound dog with bared teeth standing over him, and it took all my concentration to keep the vehicle at or under the speed limit. The last thing I wanted was to get stopped by the police for speeding. Another concern was that Stretch might break free and bash me over the head. But he was bound so tightly he couldn't move. Even then I couldn't help but check the rear view mirror every few minutes. It was "All Quiet on the Western Front". You remember how the movie ended? I hoped my quiet night would end the same way for Stretch and not for me.

After a while, on the way to the monastery, I relaxed for the first time during that evening. My breathing slowed, and I had not suffered an anxiety heart attack. That's always a worry for a guy my age, although unfounded, as I'm in good health despite the two packs a day cigarette habit.

I reviewed the entire event in my mind to see if anything went wrong and everything seemed to go as planned. There was no blood spilled during the kidnapping, so I never needed the carpet, and I thought it might be a good idea to keep it since it was still in pristine condition. I hate to waste money, and the carpet might be useful to keep dirt off my vehicles carpet if I went to the nursery for some shrubs. But my better judgment kicked in. I could not face my fellow cellmates if I told them I got caught because I wouldn't get rid of a twenty-dollar piece of carpet. Inwardly I smiled again. Sick sense of humor, I guess.

****

The trip to the monastery was uneventful. There was very little traffic at that time of night and the weather turned to scattered showers, just enough rain to keep people indoors on a miserable night. I pulled up to the main gate and saw that the broken padlock was still in place meaning that in all likelihood I was the last person there. Nothing was disturbed. I removed the damaged padlock, drove the Land Rover through the gate, and replaced the lock. There was always the possibility a security guard or a patrol car cop might have the monastery grounds on his route, but it would be unusual for a guard to enter the premises unless he saw the lock removed, or something amiss.

I drove to the garage with the lights out, parked the van under a tall leafy Banyan tree, unlocked the rear hatch and escorted Stretch out of the vehicle, and through the front door, all the while assuring him that he would not be hurt provided he did not resist. I reminded him that he was still blindfolded and had never seen my face so I had no reason to hurt him. He believed me and followed my directions to a tee without hesitation, although he must have been scared shitless.

I had brought along a battery powered lantern for illumination and led Stretch to a solid oak high back office chair, vintage about 1960, when furniture was made to last a lifetime, and had him straddle the chair so his chest was against the back rest. I then ducat taped his body to it using half a roll of tape. His hands were still bound behind his back with plastic ties, and I taped his arms to his body and around the back of the chair using a few feet of ducat tape, but leaving his hands exposed. There was a reason for this, for leaving his hands and fingers exposed, and I'll get to that in a moment. He could not get free regardless of how hard he might try. He wasn't going anywhere on his own volition. He was going to stay on the property for a very long time, for all eternity if all went well. Next I covered the single window with a small heavy blanket, opened the garage doors, drove the Land Rover into the building, shut the door, flopped into a chair, and contemplated the sequence of the next moves. Everything had to be orchestrated just right for the interrogation to go smoothly

When all the preparations had been made I went to the SUV and retrieved the thermos. It was filled with coffee, now lukewarm, but still better than nothing. I sure didn't want to stop off at a Dunkin Donuts on the way to the monastery therefore I had to make do with what I had. For some reason I wanted a cigarette even though I gave up smoking after the Ouija board session, so I searched Stretch's pockets and sure enough he had a pack of Marlboro's. I took one out and smoked it with the coffee, and thought about how I was going to handle this. A good cigarette with a cup of coffee always helps me think clearly, and what the hell, one cigarette wouldn't hurt.

After a few minutes I removed the gag but not the blindfold and said,

"I know what you do for a living, but I don't know your name. Will you please tell me?"

"Go fuck yourself" he replied.

Maybe I was too easy on him, making him feel too comfortable by assuring him that he would not be hurt. *He thinks I'm some sort of pussy. Well he's in for a surprise.*

"Now that's no way to answer me. I'm trying to be polite, please tell me your name"

"I told you, it's "go fuck yourself.""

I didn't say anything, and replaced the gag. Stretch was silent again and still sightless. I didn't want him to see what was about to happen, and I had no idea if his screams would be loud enough to alert anyone. No sense in taking chances.

I went to my bag of tools and removed the bolt cutter, and smiled to myself thinking this was going exactly as I thought it would, and said,

"OK, we want to play games do we?"

I had previously run this scenario through my mind, and was ready for it. I had hoped his being uncooperative would give me the excuse to proceed to more aggressive means to get compliance. Now he was giving me an excuse to do so.

I removed two plastic garbage bags from the tool kit and taped one around my waist turning it into a makeshift apron, and cut face and arm holes into the second bag turning it into a poncho. The poncho went over my head and upper torso. It looked like a plastic hooded sweatshirt. Keeping blood off my clothing was a must. Stained clothing would render it unusable, and even though I would never wear the suit again it was going into the church poor box after this nights work. Doing good deeds makes for good Karma.

Strange things are happening. Now I'm smoking again and thinking of doing good charitable work by donating my clothes to the less fortunate. What the hell?

After finishing the coffee I walked over to Stretch, and placed the bolt cutter over his pinky finger being careful not to contact any skin. I wanted this to be a complete surprise. I then squeezed the handle with all my strength. The finger came off as cleanly as a rose bud cut with garden shears. And to my surprise, there wasn't even that much blood. I really didn't need the garbage bag uniform. *Oh well, after all, this is a learning experience, and it's prudent to be as careful as possible.*

I wish I were able to see Stretch's eyes and hear him scream when the finger was lopped off, but he was still blindfolded and gagged. All I heard was a muffled cry, albeit a loud one. If the gag was not in place he could have awoken the dead. After a few minutes his cries diminished into soft whimpering sounds. I kept quiet all the while. Sometimes silence is more effective than speech. He finally settled down and must have realized that I meant business. I gave him a few more minutes to fully digest what had happened, and then removed the gag but left the blindfold on.

"OK" I said, "you now have nine fingers, want to go for eight?

"What! Are you crazy?" he sobbed.

"No, I don't think so, but maybe I am" I replied.

"You said you wouldn't hurt me."

"Well I have been known to lie. But let's move on. What is you name? And don't say its "go fuck yourself."

"It's Ralph Kinder"

"That's better. Did you know that "Kinder" in German means child, and you have been acting like a child? Didn't your mother tell you that when a boy does bad things he gets punished?"

Ralph began to sob and tremble. My tone was like Hannibal Lector's. It was designed to frighten him and it was working. His crotch and the front of his trousers were wet and a puddle was forming at the bottom of his pants leg. He was ready to talk, to spill his guts, and give me the answers I was looking for. I really did not want to torture him. I did not relish the job of extricating information this way. But in the long run it would save a lot of time and produce the least amount of blood.

"OK, "Now that you know I am not some pussy asshole so let's get down to business. You still have not seen my face so if I get the answers I want you might get out of this alive. To start with, what kind of drugs are you selling?"

"Just weed"

I said nothing, went to the workbench, picked up the bolt cutter, and took off another finger. He howled like a banshee.

Good thing we are away from civilization, his wailing could cause a problem.

When Ralph quieted down I said,

"Ralph, you know you only have eight fingers now. If I get nine wrong answers I'll have to cut off your pecker."

"I'm selling coke" he sobbed "and sometimes pills."

"That's better, maybe now we can have a truthful dialogue. Next question, who is your supplier?"

"I really don't know his name. Nobody uses real names but they call him Escarabajo. I think it means beetle in Spanish, maybe because it's hard to kill a beetle."

"OK Ralph, now we're getting somewhere. So tell me all about how you arrange to get the shit, and where do you pick it up?"

Ralph didn't want to get to the ninth wrong answer so he told all without holding anything back. I found out the location of the warehouse where he picked up his supply, and any details he was aware of, like do they pay off any cops, their hours of operation, when the warehouse was vacant – which was never, and what type of security they had in place.

The interrogation over, and wanting to finish up my business as quickly as possible, I retrieved from my bag of goodies a piece of leather fashioned out of an old belt. The belt had a ¾ inch steel nut, a nut that would normally be screwed on to a bolt, taped to the inside of the leather strap. Without alerting Ralph, as he was still blindfolded and couldn't see what I was doing, I carefully placed the belt over his head and around his throat with the nut facing his carotid artery. Then, standing behind him, I pulled the belt back with all the strength I had and all the force I could muster. Ralph's reaction was as if I had placed his finger in an electric lamp socket and plugged it into 220 volts. He jolted up, tried to kick and struggle, but he was bound securely to the chair, and the chair was secured to the table, so his struggle was short and futile. When the blood supply is cut off from the brain it only takes a few seconds for a person to lose consciousness. But I wasn't taking any chances. I kept the pressure up for a few minutes until I was certain he was dead.

Everything was going just as planned. There was almost no blood to clean up, just a little from Ralph's severed fingers, and my vintage suit was still clean. I felt very strongly about being able to donate the suit to charity, and I didn't want it ruined with bloodstains.

I know I lied when Ralph was told he might live. But if he could, he would thank me for not telling him the truth. This way he didn't have as much anxiety. Dying is not so bad when you think of it. It's the anticipation we fear, not the actual process if it's relatively painless, quick and unexpected. I only hope my death will be as fast as Ralph's when the time comes. But I hope it's at age ninety-five, and I'm in bed sleeping at the time.

All the loose ends were tidied up in less than a half hour. The good thing about living alone is that you become an efficient housecleaner. I sloshed the blood stained floor with Clorox. That should get rid of all the blood and DNA evidence. Then I removed the cash, credit cards and all possible identification from Stretch's wallet. There was also a photo of a woman about his age. I suppose it was his girlfriend, and I hoped for her sake she makes better choices of boyfriends in the future. I kept the cash and credit cards. I could always use more cash, and the credit cards might become a valuable asset. They were worthless for getting money out of an ATM as the machines take pictures of transactions, but the cards just might come in handy some day. I burned all the other contents of his wallet. You never know when an innocuous little scrap of information can become evidence and put you away for life.

Satisfied that all the bases were covered, I dragged Ralph outside by the light of the moon, dug a shallow grave behind the building, and buried him. After the burial I reconnoitered the entire area for tell tale signs of footprints or tire tracks. There was none. When all the messy work was finished I returned to the garage, took a last look around the building to be sure nothing was overlooked, packed up the tools and other paraphernalia, changed into street clothes and silently left the monastery compound being careful to wipe down and replace the padlock when I exited. If nothing goes wrong on the way home, I thought, it will have been another perfect crime, and I felt good about it, no remorse whatsoever.

The drive back to my apartment was uneventful. I didn't encounter any cop cars nor did I run any red lights. Back home many of the traffic lights have cameras that record traffic violators, and I didn't know if there were any cameras in place in St. Petersburg, but I certainly wasn't going to risk getting photographed in an area where I would not normally visit.

Two stops had to be made on the way home, one to the church poor box to get rid of the shoes and suit, and at the Laundromat to do my weekly wash. While the clothes were being washed I drove to a dumpster to get rid of the carpet, and then discarded the bolt cutter in an empty weed infested lot which was used as an illegal dumpsite for local landscapers. I hated getting rid of the stuff, I might have to buy the same articles again, but it was for the best. There might be DNA evidence hidden in the carpet fibers, and the cutter can leave traceable cut marks on the padlock's shackle. I kept the ducat tape and a few other remaining goodies. I couldn't imagine there being any connection to Ralph's disappearance. I think I was home free.

August 12th

I returned the SUV, went back to the apartment, and took the day off. I had a lot of thinking to do for the next event, the grand finale, the act that would get a lot of drugs off the street. I know it's like pissing in the ocean. It's not going to raise the sea level, but it will make a little difference for a short while, and most of all it will make me feel good.

Ralph told me before his untimely demise where he obtained his supply of drugs, the location of the warehouse, and other pertinent information I needed to implement my plan. But first I needed a plan, so I left the apartment after breakfast and drove over to Treasure Island, a resort town on the Gulf of Mexico ten miles away from downtown St. Petersburg.

The town of Treasure Island, and it's environ is a sleepy little resort area in November and a bustling village during the winter season. Back in the day Susan and I had vacationed in the area, in St. Pete Beach. It's a great place for a vacation, famous for fine dining, and swimming in the warm Gulf water. I suppose it is also a good drop off point for drugs being smuggled in by a boat from Mexico. I wondered if the drug cartel had picked the town because of its name. Treasure Island certainly was an apt name for the white powder treasures stored on the little island.

The island is directly on the Gulf of Mexico. At the southern tip where it faces the town of St. Pete Beach there is a cut from the gulf into the protected bay on the north side of the island. Once inside the bay there are vacation homes, marinas, restaurants, and a few commercial building directly on the water. It's a perfect location for receiving shipments of contraband.

Using the van's GPS, I spotted the building Ralph had revealed to me, and slowly drove past it while making mental notes of all the details. I continued driving for another mile or so, made a U turn, and drove past it again for further observations. There wasn't any impediment that could not be dealt with or that would interfere with my plan. The warehouse was not a commercial building as I had expected. It was just a residential home on the bay with a slip for mooring a fairly large boat.

It was now mid-day and my stomach growled telling me it wanted some food. So I consulted the GPS, found a nearby restaurant for lunch, and drove to it.

After considering all the good work that I had accomplished in the last few days I felt the need to reward myself with a hardy meal. A cheeseburger, some French fries, and a genuine full flavored beer sounded like a good idea. To hell with a turkey burger; I have not one, but two hungry spirits inside me and they both want real beef. I'm sure they will keep my body healthy for their own well being.

***

The restaurant turned out to be a homey place on the waterfront, just the kind I prefer. It was a one story wooden building built back in the sixties with a deck overlooking the water, and a dock for transient boats. I hate the new glass and granite restaurants they call diners. Give me an old fashioned eatery with a dozen red vinyl padded stools facing the serving counter and comfortable booths lining the front of the building. An old-fashioned jute box in the corner playing do-op records would also be nice, but you seldom find them any more.

I found a booth by a window facing the bay. The waitress came over, greeted me in a friendly voice, presented a menu, and left giving me time to read the fare of the day. I already knew what I wanted - a burger, so I skipped reading the menu and stared at the moored boats which bobbed up and down in the water, as they reacted to the wake of the motor boats passing by. It was a pleasant moment that I would be sure to remember. It was nice to enjoy the moment and think about nothing of consequence for a while.

The waitress shattered the mood when she showed up for my order.

"Hi" she said, "you look like your having a good day."

"Yes," I said, still smiling. "And how are things with you today?"

"Great," She replied, "Are you new in town? I haven't seen you here before, and I know just about everyone during the off season."

"Yep, I'm thinking of doing a little fishing for a few days."

"Well if you get a nice Grouper bring it in and the cook will fix a great meal."

"Sounds good, but if I land something big like a Marlin, I'm having it stuffed."

"I hope you do. It's good for business. A big catch like that brings out the fisherman. Right now the entire island is like a ghost town."

Yeah, and I'm going to add a few more ghosts.

We continued to banter back and forth for a while. Business was slow. The restaurant only had a few occupied tables, and she was not pressured to tend to other patrons for the moment. They had already been served, and not ready for a refill on their drinks so she had time to chat. I asked about the economy and how it affected the restaurant business. Every one wants to talk about the economy these days. Misery likes company. She said it's slow with the kids getting ready to go back to school, but it should pick up in the fall when the snowbirds come down. Meanwhile, the town was almost empty, lots of vacant houses, and not much traffic. The motels were offering deep discounts. All the local merchants were scrambling for whatever business there was.

I filed all this information in my head for use a few days hence, and ordered lunch, a big juicy burger topped with raw onion, lettuce and tomatoes. The rabbit food, the lettuce and tomato topping added to the burger was the healthy portion of the meal. But I counteracted the health food with a large order of greasy French fries and a Heineken. There is nothing like junk food to satisfy a big guy.

I always think more clearly on a full stomach so while putting away the burger I thought of what was learned about the warehouse, and what I would have to find out before attempting to destroy it. I know the warehouse is actually a one family, two-story wood shingled building with a six-foot vinyl covered metal cyclone fence surrounding the entire property. Very few homes in the area had fences but a sturdy fence would not seem out of place for this home because there was a dog, a nasty looking Pit Bull who roamed loose on the grounds. I didn't think a breeder who supplies animals for a petting zoo trained him. I also had to find out what security measures were in place. There were cameras on the fence, obviously used for surveillance, but were the cameras supplemented with motion sensors or other electronic devices that might detect trespassers? This is going to take a lot more investigation before I can proceed with my plans. This is not going to be a piece of cake.

The thought, "it's not a piece of cake", reminded me to get back to the business at hand, eating the burger before it got cold.

***

When I returned to my apartment I searched the newspaper for any news about Ralph. There was only one article in the paper concerning a death. It was about two children who died in a house fire. News of that sort disturbed me because if the family had only invested in a smoke detector the kids would still be alive. There was also an article about a car crash, a pile up on the interstate, and it killed the driver. News like that didn't bother me at all. People drive too fast, and if they demolish their cars and get killed in the process, it's their own fault. There was also a drug related drive by killing, but nothing about Ralph. I suppose when there is no body there is no crime. In Ralph's case all the police have is an abandoned car with some coke on the street. It's hardly worth mentioning.

I was tempted to drive by the abduction site to see if his car was still there but thought better of it. After all, what would it have accomplished? If his car was gone it might mean the police found it and had it towed. If it was still there I might be tempted to stop and examine the site to see if I left any telling clues. And if the car was under surveillance I would be nabbed and interrogated. I decided to let sleeping dogs lie. If I'm a suspect I'll find out about it soon enough, so I put the entire subject out of my mind.

Later on that evening I once again gave it some thought. I wondered how I could be so calloused as to dismiss the killing without even a pang of remorse.

August 13th

I got up early, skipped breakfast and went to the park in the hope of picking up a tennis game. I was in luck; the men I met the week before were there, and they had brought along another player. We paired up; I went with the strongest player because being a newcomer I was an unknown quantity, and in the event I proved to be a rank amateur compared to the other players, my partner could carry me. But it turned out okay. I didn't embarrass myself. In fact my partner and I won both sets although not by a great margin. The scores were 6-4, 6-3.

Afterwards we sat around the cement checkers table, and shot the breeze for a while. We talked about tennis and I was flattered when my partner asked if I would be at the courts the next day. I replied with an enthusiastic yes. Believe me, there is no better compliment for a tennis player than being asked to play again. Of course we talked about football. Everyone talks football in St. Petersburg. And it's not only the Buccaneers they talk about. Friday night high school football rivals the NFL here. Football in any shape or form is a state passion. The conversation finally got around to me. My new friends wondered where I was for the past few days, if I fell off the ends of the earth or something. Very funny, everybody's a jokester.

I made an excuse and told them I had sprained my ankle stepping off the curb at the mall. This pacified them, but it got me to thinking, in my new line of work where I could not account for my time I would have to be careful not to make too many friends. A month ago when I had the new ethereal spirit controlling my life, and before the two spirits came to a compromise, being totally self-sufficient didn't bother me. In fact I preferred being alone with my consuming anger and hatefulness. But now things were different. I wanted some friends. The kitten wasn't enough. More of my old personality was surfacing. Is this a good or bad thing; am I getting a conscience? Does this mean I will stop killing or will I continue killing just for the fun of it?

After tennis, and the idle chitchat I went home and pissed away the day like I usually do. That's what's great about not having any responsibilities other than the new project of eliminating a small link to the drug trafficking in St. Petersburg. Back home, and I am talking about back in New York, I would be helping with the housework, as Susan kept busy running the family business. I would run errands, pick up the mail at the Post Office, shop at the supermarket, and go to the drugstore for our daily ration of cigarettes. We never purchase a carton of smokes, only two or three packs at a time because we were always saying we would quit in a day or two when the latest crises was over, and Susan wasn't so tense. But that never happened. When you own a small business there is a crisis almost every day. When people lecture me about the evils of cigarettes and ask: "When are you going to quit smoking? It's going to kill you" I always say, "Yeah, I'm quitting, and it's easy to quit. I've quit smoking a hundred times."

And I finally did give up the filthy habit in the time it takes to blink an eye on the day my new spirit took over. There were no withdrawal cravings. I didn't have to take pills or placebos, wear patches or chew nicotine gum because the new "me" never smoked. I did have one or two cigarettes in the last few months but I never enjoyed them. I suppose I just wanted to experiment and see if they still had a hold on me, and they did not. I was finally cured. That is, I was a non-smoker until the night I got rid of Ralph. On the night I ended Ralph's life I drank a cup of coffee while considering how to precede with the mission, and I needed a smoke to help me think clearly, so I riffled through Ralph's pockets and dug out one of his smokes, and enjoyed it while downing the coffee. Obviously it was the old me exerting its will. There must be a hell of a battle going on inside my body.

Now I am back to smoking a pack a day and struggling to keep the habit from increasing to two packs a day. This nicotine addiction is clearly an indication of my two souls compromising with each other, each one giving up a little control over my life for the sake of harmony. It's a good thing they are learning to live with each other or I might end up in a mental facility for the incurably insane for the rest of my life.

**

There is additional evidence of my morphing into a new person. First of all, I don't curse as much as before, but the really big change is one I'm really happy about.

Last night after I went to bed, in the middle of the night, I awoke with an erection for the first time in a very long time.

I never gave it much thought before, in fact I never gave it any thought but I have been sexless, like a eunuch, and have not had physical relations with a woman since my personality changed. In retrospect I don't think I have had an erection either.

It's interesting to note that one of the impotence tests is to observe a man while asleep overnight in a controlled environment, in a sleep center. If he does not have an erection at least once during that time period he is physiologically impotent.

Not only did I have a strong hard-on but it was accompanied by a dream. I dreamt that Susan and I were on a Caribbean Island, all alone on a deserted beach, and we were both stark bare assed naked. Susan was at an age when we first met. She was slim and sexy, and I was young, handsome and thirty pounds lighter. We looked like young models right out of a fashion magazine, and in fact, Susan was offered a job as a model when she was younger, and if I say so myself, I was actually quite handsome. I won't go into details but needless to say, in the dream we had some great sex.

Sex is something I am starting to think about again. I never cheated on Susan and haven't had a girl friend for so long I'm not sure how to strike up a conversation with a woman. I'll have to ask Ray. He's an expert about such things and is on his third wife. Maybe he or one of my new found tennis buddies could arrange a mixed doubles match with some single females. No, that may not be a good idea. Aside from possibly complicating my mission any women my friends knew would most likely be the same age as me and I didn't want that. If I got a girlfriend she had to be no older than fifty, and forty is better yet. At my age I might have a virility issue that only a young woman can cure. Maybe I'd go online and order a bride from Russia or from the Philippines. That way I could purchase a twenty-five year old beauty. I knew one guy who sent away for a Russian girl and he had some great sex for six months. Six months was the amount of time the bride needed to get her green card, or whatever documentation she needed to stay in this country.

My friend knew he was being used by the girl but he didn't care. It was great fun while it lasted.

Jeez! Listen to me, this must be the new me talking. I never would have spoken about women this way a year ago. I might have momentary thoughts, or kidded about getting a mail order bride, but that's as far as it goes. Besides, when it comes right down to it, I would never spend that kind of money. So I guess I'll have to find a girl friend here in St. Petersburg or follow Woody Allen's advice. One of his funny one-liners was: "There's nothing wrong with masturbation. It's having sex with the one you love the most."

Aug 23rd.

I awoke early this morning, went to the tennis court, and picked up a game with my new buddies. Afterwards we sat around the checkers table and talked for a while. The subject zeroed in on politics. The old timers on the East coast are for the most part Democrats but here on the West coast there are more Republicans. I guess that's because the Palm Beach and Ft. Lauderdale retirees are from New York while the West coast of Florida is home to Mid-Westerners and Canadians. It's amazing to see the difference in the cultures. It's liberal vs. conservatives.

When the guys asked me my political affiliation I was stumped for a minute. I had to think about it. The subject of politics had not crossed my mind since

I left New York. I used to be a liberal Democrat and I'm not sure what I am now.

At one time I supported and contributed to the Democratic Party. I thought everyone was entitled to free medical care and equal opportunity. Well, I supported universal health for selfish reasons, so I guess that doesn't count. It cost a ton of money for our employee's medical coverage and I wish the government would pick that up. But as far as the rest of the Democratic platform goes, I was with it all the way.

And I suppose I am a Republican now, although I'm not sure why. I'm not rich anymore. I certainly don't pay any taxes, and the Republican Party is generally considered the affiliation for those who are rich or think they may soon be wealthy. Maybe I am a Republican because the person I became after the Ouija session didn't give a damn for the little guy who is struggling to get by. I didn't care if he was out of work, and on the verge of losing his house through foreclosure. But now I was beginning to get more compassionate again, so I am not sure what my political affiliations are. It's all very confusing. What I do like about the Republican Party though is their hands off attitude, States Rights, and especially their stand on gun control.

When the tennis group tired of talking about politics and what's wrong with this country, the rising property taxes and the lack of jobs in Pinellas County I brought up a topic which I should have left alone. Even though I knew it was the wrong thing to do I brought up the subject of my not having a girl friend, and did they know of any available single women. I should have known better, but I was getting very horny and not thinking of the possible ramifications. I should have taken my time and searched the Internet for a dating website, or just gone to a local pub on a Friday night. There are always plenty of girls in a local bar at the end of a workweek. That's when most guys get paid, and they are more apt to open their pocket to buy a single girl a drink or two, and the girls are well aware of that fact.

All my friends had a friend, or a friend of their wife who knew of a single girl or a widow looking to meet someone. If there is one thing St. Petersburg has more than enough of -- its widows, and old maid single females, and I was an old bull ready for the slaughterhouse, a very desirable commodity. Maybe I should pin a price tag on my shirt and sell myself to the highest bidder.

I listened to all my buddy's offers and selected Ray's second cousin's wife. Ray's relationship with the woman was far enough removed so if things didn't work out, and if she got hurt, it wouldn't affect our friendship. I mentioned this concern to Ray and he was OK with it. He was on his third wife so hurting women was nothing new to him.

The middle aged cousin-in-law had lost her husband to a heart attack six months earlier and was eager to start dating again. She owned a house about a mile away from my apartment, and had a job at the local Publix as a cashier. Not a great position, but she probably received a discount on all her food purchases. That had to help with her budget. What Ray didn't tell me was that his cousin-in-law was in financial trouble. I found out later that her husband was a welder at a local foundry and made a fair wage. But it was a non-union job, and he had neither a pension that could be passed on, nor a personal retirement plan, and the house was not paid for. She must have been desperate to find a husband before the money ran out. I had news for her; it wasn't going to be me.

And so it was that I let Ray fix me up. Sheila, that was her name, invited me over to her house for dinner. I'm sure she wanted to show me her best qualities: that she was a great cook and not a gold digger, or a princess wanting to be wined and dined at an expensive French restaurant. By the way, a ploy like that wouldn't work for me. That's how I got hooked into my marriage with Susan. Not that it was a bad thing because I loved Susan dearly throughout our long marriage, but that's how she first got me interested, through my stomach with home cooked meals.

The date with Sheila was set for the coming Saturday night. I looked forward to it but in the meanwhile I had to proceed with what I now called "My Mission".

I was in no rush to complete the mission. Sometimes anticipation of an event is better than the event itself. For example, there have been times when Susan and I booked a cruise to the Caribbean with friends, and the booking took place several months before the actual sailing date. This gave us the opportunity to meet with the other couple to select the date, the cruise line, and side trips we might take once we disembarked at our island destination. I always want to go snorkeling and Susan usually goes along with my choices, but our friends are not swimmers, so we have to decide what side trips we would do together, and those we would do separately. This always leads to more decisions: do we meet for dinner onshore after our respective side trips or do we go to a late dinner onboard the ship? I can go on and on but needless to say when you travel with other people, planning a trip is not easy, but it's fun. It's fun to plan things and get excited over the upcoming event. In the winter you can put up with the cold and snow because you know that in a few weeks you will be basking in the sunshine. The reality though is that the cruise might turn out to be a disaster. Once we were on a cruise ship that had a norovirus outbreak and we were all quarantined on the ship. That was a bummer.

Getting back to the mission: first thing was to formulate a plan and make notes as to what I knew about the drug ware house, and what I had to do to destroy it and wipe it off the face of the earth. I knew it was a waterfront home, with a dock on Boca Ciega Bay, and it was close to the inlet separating Madeira Beach Island from Treasure Island. I knew the house was enclosed with a fence, and a large, vicious unleashed Pit Bull prowled the enclosure. I knew that breaching the security system and getting into the house undetected was not going to be easy. I knew I had a very tough job on my hands.

It's easy to enumerate the problems. What is not easy is finding solutions. But after awhile it finally came to me. I didn't have to get into the building; I just had to destroy it.

***

Thank God for the Internet; you can find anything online. I searched "bomb making" and found a site that will sell you plans and show you how to take down the Empire State Building if you so desired. Problem was -- you had to use a credit card for the purchase of the plans, and if the FBI or Homeland Security has any brains they probably monitor the site. I sure don't want to get on their watch list so I kept searching. What I did find though is bomb making ingredients. Someone who was not afraid of dying could construct a bomb from scratch and use the trial and error method. All you need is potassium nitrate, charcoal, and sulfur, and you can purchase the ingredients online or at a local supply house. Any nut job can blow up anything. And congress worries about gun control? I think they should evaluate their priorities and do something to control the Internet, and the sale of hazardous material, but not until I complete my mission.

After a little more searching I discovered that I could very easily blow myself up making a bomb so I gave up that notion. I'll leave bomb making to the Islamic terrorists. They don't give a damn if they die attempting to fabricate explosives as seventy-two virgins await them in paradise. Now that's being greedy. I would settle on just two or three young virgins. What I did find out though is that I could buy mortars, rockets, and explosive fireworks of all kinds right here in Florida, in Tampa, a few miles from my home. What a great state I moved to. You can get guns, make bombs and do whatever you like to do in Florida.

August 26th

After fixing breakfast for myself and Kitty I left town for Tampa. It was about 9:00 AM during what the locals call the rush hour, and what we New Yorkers call a nice morning drive, and drove to the fireworks store on Flagler Street, off Interstate 275. I needed to buy the explosive material to wipe the drug house off the face of the earth.

The selection of things that go bang, sizzle, soar into the air, and burst into an array of sparks was mind-boggling. Grucci's 4th of July spectacular back in New York City could be duplicated if you wanted to spend the money. I didn't have that kind of cash, but I was willing to part with enough greenbacks to blow up a drug warehouse.

August 28th

It's Saturday and I had to get ready for my date with Sheila. I wanted to look my best so after a leisurely breakfast with Kitty I went down to the pool to get a healthy glow on my face, and Kitty does what she does best, she went back to sleep. I relaxed all day and took a nap in the afternoon. I had to conserve my energy in the unlikely event I might get lucky and get laid. Stranger things have happened to me.

I awoke from my nap about 5:00 PM, showered, shaved, and left for the much anticipated dinner date with Sheila. I had no idea as to where she lived so I entered her address into the Nissan's GPS navigation system, took a last look into the rear view mirror to make sure the little hair I have was neat and tidy, and took off for her house.

The route took me into an older neighborhood, a shabby sub development, and it was definitely a blue collar area. Doubts were forming in my mind as to the wisdom of this date. I located her home, parked at the curb and hesitantly walked up to the front door proceeding very slowly because I was seriously considering turning around and going home. As I approached the house I noticed the paint was peeling from the one story cinder block and stucco home. *Wait till I get my hands on Ray for fixing me up with this dirt bag redneck. He is going to pay dearly for this blind date.* But as they say, "in for a penny, in for a pound", so I rang the bell.

When the door swung open I stood there mute for a second. I was taken aback. Sheila was a knock out beauty. I was dumbfounded. She was in her mid fifties, but looked ten years younger. She was slim but curvaceous, and exuded a primitive sensuality even a blind man could sense. Her angelic face was framed with flowing blondish hair that curled under at her shoulders, and her eyes were a deep pool of blue. I had to thank Ray for this date when I saw him.

Sheila escorted me into her living room and offered me a drink before dinner. I had a martini and she had a gin and tonic. The drink helped me to relax and digest my good luck; she probably had a drink to be social.

We sat in her living room getting acquainted and making small talk. I lied about my past life and she probably told me the truth about hers. I looked around at the surroundings as we talked. The house was a small but comfortable home consisting of three bedrooms. It was tastefully done in hues of soft brown and amber. You could tell immediately that this girl was no trailer trash as I had first suspected.

After a while we moved into a dining alcove off the kitchen and Sheila served a fantastic meal of roast beef with all the fixings. I had not had a meal like that since I left New York, and was impressed. We talked, had coffee and cake, and talked some more. Finally it was time to go home. I asked her for a date for the following Saturday and to my amazement she said yes. I kissed her goodnight, floated down the steps in a state of euphoria, and went home never even trying to have sex with her. This girl was a keeper and I was not going to embarrass myself and get rejected right off the bat. She was a recent widow, and I was her first date after the death of her husband. I sensed that we both had to take it slowly. I haven't ad sex in such a long time another week or so wouldn't matter.

On the way home I reflected on the evening. Sheila was a lovely, mature woman. All the negative thoughts I had about her were erroneous. She was happily married for a long time to a good man, a hard working husband who did the best he could for his family on his limited salary. Sheila had raised two good boys; both of them were out of the house and happily married. I thought to myself that I had to learn to be more compassionate, and less of an elitist jerk, and had no right to pre-judge anyone. I was a pompous ass of the first degree. But maybe I can change.

August 29th

The first order of business was to get on the computer and surf the Internet for an unpopulated area to assemble and test the explosive devices. I planned to construct a bomb or some sort of weapon capable of completely destroying the drug house using components extracted from the fireworks purchased in Tampa. But first I had to make sure the goodies would do their job and I would not get blown to hell. Map Quest indicated a suitable testing ground in the middle of the state and I clicked on Google Earth to see the terrain, to see if it was remote enough, and far from civilization so the tests could take place without being observed by someone in the area. The Central Swamp Preserve turned out to be the perfect spot. It's a vast track of land in the middle of the state and set aside for Florida wildlife. Much of it is wooded, although not as dense as the forests in the Northeast, states like Vermont and New Hampshire. Some areas of the preserve are swampland, other sections are wooded and other parts are open meadows. Lastly, I checked out the roads leading to and from the preserve. If something went wrong it would be prudent to have an escape route.

***

I left the apartment after carefully packing up the explosives in a Styrofoam cooler. You can never be too careful. One never knows when things can go wrong. The first stop was to a gas station to fill the tank. It was going to be a long trip. Then I headed east to the preserve, and after a drive of several hours arrived at the destination. It was in the sparsely populated part of the state. As a former New Yorker, to me, it was in the wilderness. A road marker and a small sign with flaking paint indicated the entrance. There was no ranger station, snack bar, rest room or any indication that this was indeed a public park. Even the roads were unpaved, just hard packed dirt.

I drove several miles on rough dirt roads which turned into little more than cow paths before finally arriving at the testing ground. It had to be deep in the woods, where the wild animals lived and people did not. While driving into the park I had mental images of the movie *Deliverance,* and of Ned Beatty being raped by Georgia hillbillies. I might be a bit love starved and anxious for some sex, but being raped was not my idea of a good time. I was glad I brought the shotgun. It was an afterthought, and I took it with me because there are wildcats, alligators, and God knows what else that might be lurking behind every bush. I'm a city boy and not very comfortable around animals more ferocious than my pet kitten.

At long last I arrived at what I thought would be a good location to fabricate and test the explosives. I spread out a tarp to keep the chemicals off the damp swamp-like soil and began to assemble the necessary ingredients to make a bomb, and a separate rocket delivery system. I broke open the casings of the store bought mortar shells and separated the ingredients into incrementally small to large quantities. Then I inserted each mixture into an aluminum pipe, and placed the explosive concoction into the front end of a slightly longer and wider tube. Into this longer tube a Roman candle was inserted with the propulsion end sticking out a few inches. The finished product was an explosive rocket similar to the Katyusha rocket, aka, the Stalin Organ, used by the Soviets in World War Two. Rockets knocked the hell out of the

Germans when they abandoned the siege of the city of Stalingrad, and I hoped they would eliminate the drug warehouse just as efficiently.

I had very little choice in weaponry. I had to use projectiles because it was impossible to actually enter the property. The warehouse was always occupied, and it was enclosed with a steel cyclone fence, and security cameras were mounted on the fence posts. And worst of all was the ferocious dog. There are not a lot of things I'm afraid of but when it comes to facing down an angry Pit Bull, that's where I draw the line, so the warehouse had to be destroyed from afar. Besides, I love to watch fireworks.

Once the assembly work was completed, I found a dry patch of grass, and sat down with the now cold thermos of coffee and enjoyed a cigarette. I felt very satisfied, and viewed the explosives with pride and a sense of accomplishment. But the big test was yet to come. I had to see if it all worked. This is one time when the expression 'I'll get it to work or die trying' might be a truism.

The first order of business was to set up an adjustable cradle, one that I had pre-fabricated the day before at my apartment. Its purpose was to secure a rocket for firing and to be able to adjust the rocket's trajectory. I started with the smallest rocket, loaded it into the cradle, set it for a low angle and lit the fuse.

Big mistake; the rocket only flew about twenty feet, nosed into the ground and exploded with the sound of a cherry bomb. It would have been OK as a first try, but the rocket, (which was really a roman candle mounted behind a small mortar) spun in circles and spewed out balls of colored fire in every direction, including my direction. I got hit in the leg before having a chance to high tail it out of there. The damage to my leg was tolerable. I didn't need all the hair on my leg anyway.

Over the next few hours I experimented with various combinations of explosives and rockets. I adjusted the angle of the cradle, and used larger rockets to have them fly further, and finally got the combination of explosives and trajectory correct through trial and error. However the devices were not reliable. When in flight they often veered out of control. Once it boomeranged and almost took me out. Eventually I had to quit for the day; it was getting dark, and I was getting frustrated. I had to go home and figure out what went wrong.

When I arrived home, and after a cold bottle of beer, I added fins to keep the device flying on a true and steady course, and when I was satisfied everything would work without blowing me up I called Sheila to see if she wanted to have dinner the next night. I was thinking about her a lot and didn't want to wait until the next Saturday to see her again. To my delight, she said yes. I went to sleep thinking about her and it was the first time in a long time I didn't fall asleep thinking about killing someone.

***

I woke up feeling very anxious with a sense of foreboding, a strong sense of impending disaster, and couldn't shake it. I had to get back to the swamp to finish testing the explosives but an uncomfortable feeling came over me, a feeling that this day should not be the day. Was my spirit trying to warn me of something? After all, my spirit, the one I was born with, knows the future. He has been there before. But I shook off the eerie feeling and ignored the warning; I had work to do, and after a light breakfast packed up the deadly paraphernalia and my shotgun and drove to the swamp.

While driving to the preserve I thought about my tennis buddies. They probably wondered why I had not called or showed up at the tennis court. I'll probably get the third degree again and have to make up some lame excuse. Having friends complicates your life. On the other hand since I seem to be returning to normal; maybe I can handle some friends. I haven't had one fight on the tennis court. I may even have a girl friend if she doesn't find a younger guy. Maybe all this talk about two souls in my body is a load of crap, and the thoughts of a temporarily deranged mind.

After a hard ride over dirt paths and bumpy trails I finally arrived at the remote testing grounds. I traveled the roads unnoticed except for a man, and (I suppose) his son fishing at a pond that was off the dirt road, and about a half mile into the preserve. I waved at them and they waved back. In retrospect I realized that it was a very stupid thing to do. Being anonymous has been my rule, and I broke it for an unnecessary show of friendship. I only hoped it would not come back to bite me in the ass. Getting sloppy is a sure way to get caught doing something you should not be doing.

Once at the testing ground, the same one I used the day before, I assembled the launcher and fired several rockets. The fins took a little tweaking before I was totally satisfied with the rocket's trajectory, but eventually everything fell into place. The devices held a true course, and almost all the test firings hit the target, a tree about fifty yards distant and in the middle of a grassy field at the far edge of a swampy quagmire. Maybe I could not breach the drug house's defenses like an experienced squad of marines with automatic weapons might have done, but it looked like the house could be destroyed from a distance of fifty yards; at least I hoped so.

Feeling satisfied as to how the day had progressed I started to pack up and get ready to go home. It was getting late in the day and I was mentally tired due to the anxiety of handling dangerous explosives and physically tired because I hadn't slept well the night before, so I wanted to quit and call it a day. But before I finished stowing the gear I noticed two men walking out of the swamp and heading towards me.

Suddenly I sensed danger, something didn't look right. If I were walking in the woods with a buddy we probably would be next to each other talking about the game we caught or might catch. But the men approaching me were not walking together side by side; they were separated by about twenty feet, the way one would stalk a prey, a mountain lion or a bear. I tensed up, felt a rush of adrenalin surge through my body and I became alert, ready for a possible confrontation. The lethargy I felt a moment before was gone. I was ready for action if the need arose.

The duo looked like hunters, but since this was a nature preserve they were probably poachers going after illegal game or alligators. In either case they were doing something illegal. The men were in their forties, and dressed in water waders, the type of waterproof gear that allows you to go waist deep into a swamp without getting wet. They had ruddy complexions and a two or three day growth of beard. I thought they might have been away from home for several days camping out and doing the macho stuff that men do. They looked scruffy but harmless enough except for the rifles they carried.

As they approached I noticed they had widened the distance between themselves by another ten feet. I was slowly being outflanked. This made me even more aware that something was not quite right, but fortunately it also made me more alert.

I intentionally remained kneeling on the ground, packing up the gear alongside the explosives and the shotgun. If I had to reach out for the gun this was a better position to be in instead of standing upright. One of the men came within a few feet of me. I looked up at him, the picture of innocence. I wasn't looking for trouble but was ready if it came my way.

The man towered over me. He looked down, his eyes avoiding mine, and said in a shaky voice,

"Hey, whatcha doing?"

His uneasiness made me even more wary. What was he so nervous about?

"Oh, just testing out some fireworks for the kids."

"Yeah, we heard the noise."

"Well I'm wrapping it up now and headed home, what are you guys doing?"

I was stalling for time - thinking about what might come next – considering options - when out of the corner of my eye I saw the other man shoulder his rifle. It looked to be a 30-06, definitely not a gun to hunt a rabbit or small game unless you wanted a meal of shredded meat. He was about twenty yards away and next to my SUV.

Suddenly a loud report sounded; the noise was his gun being fired. *The bastard shot out the rear tire of my car.* I instinctively rolled to the side, reached for my shotgun, and came to rest in a prone position with the weapon aimed at the shooter. A cartridge had previously been chambered into the shotgun and the safety was off. I always keep it off, dangerous habit I know but in this instance it probably saved my life. Without a second thought I squeezed off a round and saw the man spin sideways, his rifle flying out of his hand. I knew he would be out of action so I immediately turned my attention to the man standing over me. He was in the process of raising his gun to the firing position and it was coming to rest pointing at my head. I heard him say,

"Oh shit". His finger was on the trigger but the gun didn't fire. The safety was still engaged, and he fumbled with the lever trying to release it. A split second was all I needed to chamber another round, and I swung my shotgun towards him choosing the largest target, his chest, and squeezed the trigger. He flew backwards landing on his back. He didn't even twitch. He was dead as a doornail.

I scrambled to my feet and ran to the first guy, the one who shot out my tire. He was standing there like a dummy, more concerned with his wounds than trying to kill me before I killed him.

Before leaving St. Petersburg I had pre-loaded my gun with buckshot, small pellets which spread out as they travel, and the man and I were roughly 20 yards apart. At this distance the lead shot had a circular pattern of roughly eighteen inches in diameter, and you didn't need a direct hit to have an effective shot. It's a good thing because my shot was a foot off target. The blast caught the shooter high and to the right side of his body. His shoulder was splattered with blood, most likely his collarbone shattered, and his right ear was shredded and dripping blood on the ground. His right eye was gone; mucus looking material oozed down his face.

I ran to the dumbfounded shooter and quickly kicked his gun out of reach. Not that I had to, he couldn't have picked it up anyway. His arm was useless. It hung by his side like a slab of raw beef dangling from a meat hook. The man stood there choking back sobs and said,

"Why did you shoot me?"

"Why did you shoot out my tire?" I replied,

"We only wanted to rob you, not kill you. I shot out the tire so you couldn't drive out of here. It would take time for you to get help, and it would give us more time to get away."

"Well I'm sorry about that, I'm really sorry I had to shoot you, but what's done is done, and I can't take it back."

I was silent for a moment considering my options. I hadn't any, and finally said,

"Sorry but I can't let you out of here alive now".

Without another thought I leveled my gun at his chest, and blew him away. It was a déjà vu moment. Like I had done this before, and actually I had done this before. It was a carbon copy of the killing a few minutes earlier. The man flew backwards and landed with a thud, dead as a hog hanging from a hook in a butchers shop.

After the killing I sat down with my back against a tree and finished the thermos of cold coffee with a cigarette. I couldn't believe how relaxed and calm I felt after what should have been (to a normal person) such an unnerving experience. But the only thing that went through my mind was a funny one-liner from an old Laurel and Hardy movie, *another fine mess you got us into Ollie,* and I laughed out loud. I was really enjoying the moment. Maybe I'll call my new spirit Ollie and the old one Stan. As I remember the movie it was always Ollie who seemed to get Stan in trouble.

I also thought it was very fortuitous that Ollie encountered the poachers otherwise Stan might be pushing up daisies. Ollie is the spirit who wants to live and who is comfortable killing someone without feeling guilt or remorse and on that day it was a good thing. I'm glad he knew how to take care of himself in a dangerous situation. He must have been a hit man somewhere in time.

After finishing the coffee, I cleaned up the mess. I searched the men's pockets, removed their wallets and kept the cash and credit cards but I did not take their identification. If they were ever found at least the authorities could identify them so they could have a proper burial. I then dragged the two bodies into the swamp choosing a spot that had standing water and a depth of roughly two feet. My thought was that an alligator might eliminate the tell-tale incriminating evidence. But I couldn't count on an animal feasting on the bodies. I had to assume the men would be found, and I hoped it would be several days before that happened giving me time to complete my mission before complications set in.

I finished packing up my gear, placed the dead men's rifles in the storage area of my car, replaced the flat tire, and proceeded to drive out of the preserve.

***

A satellite circling the globe could scan the area and the preserve would appear as pristine and tranquil as it had been the day before. It was as if nothing happened. But I was wrong; I was to find out that more trouble was about to unfold.

The dirt road leading away from the testing ground abutted the section of the swamp where I had placed the two dead bodies, and what I saw in the watery marsh turned out to be the source of the complications.

I had entered my car and driven approximately a hundred yards towards the main highway before noticing movement in the swamp. The tall cat-tail grasses were swaying as though a strong wind was blowing in a five foot path, and the path was moving away from me. But the air was still; there was no wind. I stopped the car, exited it, and climbed on top of the roof for a better sighting. From this elevated position I could see the head of a man above the reeds, and it was moving fast towards the woods at the end of the swamp. I jumped off the roof, retrieved the rifle and climbed back on the car's roof. Hopefully there would be another victim to the day's kill. Unfortunately the man was nowhere to be seen. He must have made it to the safety of the woods. He was gone from sight, and there was nothing I could do about it.

On the way home I considered the chain of events in a sequential and logical manner. The father and son who were out fishing saw me heading into the swamp, and I foolishly acknowledged them. They could be a witness and identify me and the car. Also, I left behind a ton of incriminating evidence. I retrieved the shotgun shells but could not retrieve the fired rockets. Both the shells and the ordinance had fingerprints on them, and my fingerprints are on file somewhere due to my military service. But the worst of it all was the man in the swamp. I pieced together many scenarios concerning the stranger and the current situation, and the best one was this:

I was sure the man in the swamp, the one who got away, was a friend of the men I killed. Perhaps the three of them were just out hunting and given the opportunity for an easy theft decided to rob me because I was alone and a vulnerable helpless target. Or perhaps the man didn't want to participate in the robbery and waited on the sidelines for his buddies to rob me, to do what they felt they had to do.

Whether the scenario I put together was correct or not, I had to assume there was a witness to the events that had transpired, and the person would be able to identify me, and the license plate number of my vehicle. Bad luck indeed.

***

The bad luck had prompted me to accelerate my plans. I no longer had the luxury of time on my side. I had some thoughts about what I should do once the mission was completed, but they were all nebulous, just random thoughts. Would I stay in St Petersburg and plant roots in the community now that I had friends and perhaps a girlfriend to boot? Would I move on, a gypsy living in a furnished apartment, owning nothing nor having a home and possessions? Or would I be a gypsy moth traveling on air currents, taking me wherever the wind might blow, from one state to another, alone, never bonding with people, never caring?

By the time I reached St. Petersburg I came to a decision. An excerpt of one of my favorite books, *The Way of the Samurai* ran through my head, over and over again.

When one has made a decision to kill a person, even if it will be very difficult to succeed by advancing straight ahead, it will not do to think about doing it in a long, roundabout way. One's heart may slacken, he may miss his chance, and by and large there will be no success. The way of the Samurai is one of immediacy, and it is best to dash in headlong. Yamamoto Tsunetomo (c.1716)

So that was it. The decision was made. I would proceed with the plan and execute it immediately.

***

Before I reached my apartment I made a quick stop at a car wash. The SUV was spattered with mud from traveling through the preserve. Afterwards I went to the mall, pulled into an empty parking space next to a parked car and switched license plates. If an alert had already gone out a patrol car could not visually match my Nissan with the plates. The only thing I had to worry about was not to speed or to run a traffic light. That was the only way I could be identified while I was on the road, but there was not much of a chance in that happening. I'm a careful driver. My next worry was that the police could be waiting for me at my residence. That was more of a concern.

It was a little after 8:00 PM when I entered 10th. St, the street my apartment is on. But I didn't continue driving into the parking lot. Instead I parked on the street and walked the block and a half to the complex. No sense taking chances. The police might be waiting for me. I passed by the entrance to the apartment building and continued walking towards the parking lot.

My intention was to go through the lot to see if there were any cars that didn't belong there. This would not call attention to me as many pedestrians, even those who did not live in the building used the lot for a short cut to the convenience store on the next block. But before I entered the area I saw a full sized black Ford sedan parked on the street opposite the entrance to our complex, and two men were sitting in it. They had an unrestricted view of the building entrance and the lot. Could the police be more obvious? It made me think of a saying in the corporate world. "An employee will get promoted to his level of incompetence". If the detectives weren't so lazy and parked further down the street, got out of their car, and found a better spot for a stake out, I might be writing this from a jail cell.

I continued walking through the parking lot, exited on the next street and circled the block until I reached my car, started it up, and drove away. It looked like I'll never get to play tennis with my new friends and it looked like I'll never get a chance to get Sheila in bed. I wondered if I'd ever get laid again in this lifetime.

***

Tampa is a short drive from St. Petersburg. I took my time, adhering to the speed limit, and arrived at hotel row in less than an hour, and checked into a small seedy motel, one of the older ones that catered to in-flight transients. It was a one story building with a dozen rooms facing the parking area. Very convenient for a quick get away if the need arose. I used one of Stretch's credit cards for identification and told the clerk to hold the charge slip as I wanted to pay in cash when I checked out. That's always OK with a small non-franchised motel. They never turn down the opportunity to get a little unreported cash.

I was exhausted after the long hours of driving, and just wanted something to eat and to get to bed so I skipped having a full course dinner at the local Outback, a restaurant I truly loved, and instead had a burger at McDonalds, a place I used to truly hate. After the burger, I returned to the motel, crashed out for the night, and never slept better.

The next morning I checked out of the motel and ate breakfast at McDonalds again. I had a McMuffin sandwich and while I munched away I once again thought about how I used to hate fast food, and how I enjoyed it now. I suppose its Ollie's choice.

Feeling better with some food in my stomach I drove to the Westshore Plaza mall, the mall closest to the airport, to re-outfit myself. I didn't need a whole wardrobe, but I did need something to wear so I bought the basics, and a small suitcase to carry them in. I also purchased snorkeling gear and two tubular fishing pole cases to store the shotgun and the rifle I took from the man that was killed in the swamp. I don't know about Florida law but in New York having an exposed gun in your car might get you pulled over by the police.

The Tampa Mail Box Company was the final stop before leaving the city; it's an establishment that rents mailboxes and safe deposit boxes. I never get mail but I previously had rented a safe deposit box. That's where all the gold coins, cash, and the items I removed from the men I killed were kept, things like their identification and credit cards. The items were not trophies or mementos to be savored. I think it's sick to gloat over killings. But since I could never use my personal identification I thought I might be able to use my victims. The dead have no use for credit cards.

"Farewell Tampa and goodbye St Petersburg", I said to myself as I drove to interstate 275. I'll never see you again, and while I have some fond memories here I'm not going to miss you and I don't think you or you're police are going to miss me either.

I was off to Treasure Island to end the mission. After that it will be on to greener pastures, and I'll probably never be back to the state of Florida as well.

***

There are dozens of resort hotels and motels on Treasure Island and I could have had my pick of any one of them, and at a deep discount. All of them had vacancies. However, I didn't need a fancy resort on the Gulf side of the island, one with a Tiki bar where I could lounge around all day drinking rum punches and flirt with middle aged divorcees. I wasn't on the island for a vacation; I had work to do, and it's the kind of work I like best, so I checked into a small motel on Gulf Blvd. It wasn't directly on the water but an overnight rental was all I needed, and besides, while I did buy a bathing suit, and my plan called for me to perhaps go swimming, I didn't think I would have the time to lounge around the beach all day.

It was still early enough to make additional plans so I went to a marina that rented speedboats and checked out their inventory, and reserved an open bow-rider for the next evening. The salesman told me the boat would be great for catching weakfish. The boat had a 115 horsepower outboard motor, and it would get me to the best fishing area in "no time at all", according to the salesman. I didn't tell him that if all went well I would only need the boat for a few hours, and I didn't tell the salesman I was going after bigger game than Weakfish or Grouper.

Once again I used Stretch's ID but paid the deposit with cash. That was the prudent thing to do. I even bought the additional outrageously priced insurance. That's something I never do with auto rentals, but I didn't think the boat would be returned in the same pristine condition as when I rented it. There was no sense in having the marina suffer financially if I could prevent it with such a little extra cost to myself.

When I returned to the motel there was just enough time to take a refreshing dip in the pool before dinner. Usually I nap in the afternoon but I was too mentally excited for sleep so the swim was just the ticket to refresh me and kill an hour or two.

After the swim I showered and went to a local fish house and ordered an ice-cold martini appetizer and a grouper dinner. The fish was freshly caught that morning, and the house specialty. The meal was delicious, grilled to perfection, and I wished I was able to dine in the restaurant again the next night. But that was not going to happen. I would be long gone.

After dinner I returned to the motel and got into bed, but couldn't fall asleep right away. I missed Kitty. She always slept next to me, and the kitten's soft purring had me sleeping in minutes. I wondered what would become of her. When this business was over I would have to make an anonymous phone call to my landlord to alert him of the little kitten, how she would be alone, and probably starving once the dry food ran out. Kitty's welfare was the only thing that bothered me. I didn't give a tinker's damn for the few belongings I left behind, but the thought of my kitty starving to death was almost too much to handle.

***

I woke up the next day refreshed, alert, and ready for anything. I was as excited as a schoolboy getting ready for his first date and thought to myself, *this is finally it, the day I have been planning for*.

The plans for the day were simply to do nothing but take it easy, rest up and conserve my strength for the task ahead. I ate a simple breakfast at the coffee shop, a bagel and coffee. Afterwards I returned to the motel, changed into a bathing suit, chilled out at the pool, took a dip when the sun got to be too hot, and finally about 2:00 PM went to my room for a little TV followed by a short nap.

The alarm clock woke me up at 5:00 PM and I dressed in casual clothes suitable for a fishing trip, and packed a nylon sports bag with swim gear consisting of a bathing suit, fins, mask, and snorkel. The explosives had previously been packed up in a Styrofoam cooler in the SUV while at the wildlife preserve and I had previously hidden the rifles in the fishing rod case, so there was nothing else to prepare for. To the casual observer it looked like I was a real honest to goodness fisherman. Then I left for the marina, but first stopped off at a deli for a pastrami sandwich. The sandwich would have to do for dinner. It's not a good idea to have a full stomach if you have to go swimming afterwards, and while I was not planning for a dip in the Gulf, it just might come to that.

It was a short drive to the marina. I arrived shortly before they closed for the day, and checked in with the office. They scolded me for being so late. I reminded them that I had informed the salesman of my intention to fish at night, and that pacified the manager. I also reminded them that the salesman told me I could moor the boat at the guest dock when I returned. The boat had a meter that recorded the hours of use so it was no big deal, and they could invoice me accordingly and I would settle up with them the next day. The office didn't like the arrangement but they acquiesced to my demands. Business was slow in the fall season and I'm sure they were happy for any boat rentals that happened to come their way.

I loaded up the gear and powered out of the marina into the Gulf of Mexico headed west into the sunset, into the fishing grounds. When far enough from shore so that the boat could not be identified I cut the engine and drifted in the calm water, then changed into the bathing suit purchased the day before, and ate the light dinner while reminiscing about the many fishing trips I had made back home on the Long Island Sound. The pastrami sandwich washed down with a Coke hit the spot. Beer was off-limits. I had to be alert.

The sun was low over the horizon by the time I finished the sandwich, but it was still too early to go to the drug house, so I went to the front of the boat, the open bow section, sat on the cushioned bench seat, positioned myself facing west into the setting sun and relaxed with an after dinner cigarette. The water was calm, hardly a ripple disturbing the serene sea. The overhead sky was a lapis lazuli gemstone, its azure color streaked with threads of white. Off in the horizon were cumulous clouds above the sinking sun, and the sunlight illuminated the clouds from below casting dark gray shadows intertwined with red. I was transfixed, overwhelmed with the beauty and glory of nature's ever-changing landscape. I saw my life unfolding in the overhead panorama. I saw the blazing sun of my youth yielding to an ever-darkening blue sky, streaked with gray clouds of doubt and uncertainty. And lastly I saw the descent of the sun into darkness, but not before it went down in a blood red glory. I said to myself something our Native Americans might have said when entering into battle, "today is a good day to die."

In the hours between sunset and total darkness I motored to the bay, the mainland side of Treasure Island, and situated the boat roughly 200 yards from the drug warehouse. I turned off the motor and the running lights and drifted, not wanting to anchor in the event I had to make a fast get away. It was dark on the water. The moon was a crescent of silver, just entering it's "new moon" phase and I was blind for a few minutes. But after a while my eyes adjusted to the darkness. There was just enough light from the moon to see without the assistance of a searchlight. Conditions were just right, the sea calm, and the night clear. I couldn't ask for better. God or whoever watches over us must have been on my side.

When my night vision returned I scanned the homes facing the bay. Something was different. *Where is the house? Am I in the wrong spot, the wrong bay?* But then I realized that I couldn't discern the house because there was a yacht moored on the dock. I speculated, *was this a good thing or a bad one? No, this is not a bad thing. It's an opportunity to do some more good.* Most likely the yacht was making a delivery from the cartel in Mexico. This might be a chance to eliminate more than just the warehouse. Or should I leave the boat alone and just destroy the house. When the authorities arrived to investigate the incident they would confiscate the yacht and the State of Florida could sure use the money when the vessel was sold at auction. *No, Screw the state. I'd love to see the boat go up in flames. I'm entitled to some fun, am I not?*

The idiom, "It's time to fish or cut bait" ran through my mind, and that was the thought I had as I started up the motor and quietly, at idle speed, moved the bow rider to within fifty yards of the target property, and left the engine running, the transmission in neutral. The house was another twenty yards distant, so my firing range was no more than seventy yards, just slightly above the practice shots I had made in the nature preserve.

I set up three cradles on the deck of the boat, loaded each one, and aimed the first rocket at the patio door as this presented the largest target. I lit the fuse, stood back along the speedboat's handrail and prepared to dive overboard in the event the missile blew up in my face. But it didn't misfire. It flew straight and true. Unfortunately my movement caused the boat to rock and the rocket, while flying in a straight path, contacted the wooden structure of the house five feet to the right of the patio door. It exploded on a burst of color. Blue and white gobs of flame shot up in every direction, skyward, sideways, and into the patio. The building was afire but very little damage had been done. It was all external damage. I scrambled back to the cradle, ready to set another fuse. But the boat rocked violently back and forth. The deck was useless as a stable launch platform. I would have to hold the cradles and fire the rockets, and if something went wrong I might be aflame myself, or get my head blown off.

Throwing all caution to the wind I picked up and held the second cradle tightly to my chest, lit the fuse and aimed the rocket at the patio door. The fuse burned rapidly and spit white-hot sparks in every direction leaving little burn marks all over my face and bare body. *If I ever survive this, I'll probably look like I have smallpox.*

After what seemed to be an eternity, but was only a second or two, the patio door shattered and fell to the ground in a torrent of glass chips. An instant later the missile exploded inside the house. A swishing sound pulsated through the air as the Roman candle ignited and spewed burning fireballs throughout the room. A display of color shone through the window with blue and yellow fireballs spinning and crashing into the walls, the ceiling, and the furniture. The house was aflame, and I felt good.

I turned my attention to the yacht. It was going to be a fireball, the likes of which may never be seen again in the quiet harbor. But before I had the chance to ignite another rocket two men exited the burning building. They were running, and headed towards the dock, automatic rifles in their hands. One of them stopped, inserted a magazine into his weapon and raised his machine pistol towards me. The swamp man's rifle was at my feet but I was not about to get into a gunfight against automatic weapons. I might be foolish but I'm not entirely crazy, so I immediately engaged the transmission and pushed the throttle to full speed. The boat responded without hesitation and the acceleration threw me off my feet sending me sprawling backwards, and the rocket tumbled overboard into the water. I landed on my back, and the boat sped out of control in the general direction of the channel. Landing on my ass probably saved my life because as I started to get up the buzzing sound of bullets passed overhead, and I wisely stayed down, hugging the floorboards. Fiberglass splinters peppered my boat when it took a few hits but as luck would have it the motor was undamaged and the hull maintained its integrity. It was not going to sink. However the boat rental agency was not going to be too happy.

When the sound of gunfire ended I knew the boat was out of the shooters range and I cautiously crept back into the drivers' seat, took control of the steering wheel and headed for the open sea. After passing through the channel to the Gulf I finally relaxed and throttled the engine down to a more moderate cruising speed. There was no rush, no sense of urgency, so I turned off the engine, drifted in the calm water, and relaxed with a much needed cigarette. Smoking always calms my nerves and helps me clarify and organize my thoughts. I had a brilliant thought, and wanted to consider it further, and to think about the possible ramifications of what I was about to do.

***

The house was left in ruins. More than likely it burned to the ground, and when the police came and rummaged through the burnt out shell it would be obvious the home was in actuality a drug warehouse. This meant that any assets on the property would be subject to confiscation under the Rico Act. And what was left on the property? For one, it would be the Mercedes I saw parked in the driveway. But if the dealers had any brains they would have been long gone in the car. That left the yacht just sitting there. It would more than likely bring in well over several hundred thousand at auction, and probably even more as it looked to be worth at least a million. So what would I do in this situation if I were the drug dealer, escape in a car or sail away to a safe harbor in a million dollar yacht? I for one would choose the yacht.

So the fun and games were not over yet. I was excited, and even exuberant with the prospect of destroying the cartels boat, so I made an about face and headed back to Treasure Island. When the boat was a few hundred yards from the beach I turned off the engine and began drifting back to the shoreline with the help of the incoming tide. "Good timing" I thought, and the tide will help if I have to swim back to shore in the event things went wrong and I lose the speedboat. At one time I was a great swimmer but that was a long time ago and I hadn't done any long distance swimming in a long time, not since I was thirty years younger and twenty pounds lighter.

I retrieved the snorkel gear from the sports bag, loaded the one remaining rocket into the launcher, and waited. It didn't take long. The throaty sound of powerful engines drew nearer and there it was, a big beautiful forty-five foot yacht only fifty yards distant. The boat was traveling at slow speed due to the narrow opening of the channel into the sea. It was an easy target, and I was Jack Kennedy in his PT boat facing down the Japanese fleet, torpedoes at the ready.

When the yacht cleared the channel I started the engine and pulled behind the target, staying well behind the boats stern, and followed in its wake. From this position it was doubtful anyone aboard the boat could see me unless a lookout was posted on the open sun deck, and fortunately for the moment at least, the deck was empty; they must all be in the cabin. For the next few minutes I had nothing to do, and my thoughts began to wander. I hoped Ollie knew what he was doing. It would be a shame if he went to all the trouble of taking control of my body for such a short incarnation. But this was not the time for useless speculation. In a few minutes it would be the time for some action.

As we distanced ourselves from the shore the night grew increasingly darker. The few uncovered windows of the homes facing the beach, and the streetlights on the roadways of the town shed little pinpoints of light. Like the stars in the sky, they sparkled brightly but provided no illumination. The crescent sliver of the moon had cast enough light for an attack on the drug house, but it disappeared behind a cloud, and the night sky was starless and black as pitch. If there were other boats on the water they were invisible. On one hand the darkness gave me cover, however on the other hand I could not see if anyone on the yacht was standing lookout.

We were about a half-mile offshore when I perceived what seemed to be a light on the port side of the boat, on the walkway connecting the cabin to the sun deck. The light was too weak to be a flashlight and I presumed it to be a match lighting a cigarette or a cigar. When the light disappeared and only a soft glow remained I was sure it was a cigarette, and the glow was moving towards the stern. "Oh shit", I thought, "he is walking towards the sundeck. Even with the darkness he is bound to see the luminescence of my boat's wake." I had to do something about this, and I had to do it fast. I had a choice. Shoot him or get the hell out of there. I chose to shoot the guy. I picked up the rifle, the one I confiscated from the swamp thief, and waited until the light traveled upwards to his mouth. That was the target. When the light brightened indicating he was taking a drag I squeezed the trigger. The light dropped to the deck and I assumed the man went with it. They say smoking is a bad habit that will eventually kill you, and I guess they are right.

It was doubtful anyone heard the shot as the sound of our motors probably masked the sound of the rifle, but just to be safe I throttled back and dropped further behind the yacht. There was no sense in taking unnecessary risks if I didn't have to. And if I had to depart in a hurry, the extra distance between us might make the difference between life and death. My boat was fast but not fast enough to outrun machine gun bullets.

I waited for a few minutes to make sure the speedboat was still undetected and then I proceeded with the plan. It had to be implemented quickly as we were now over a half-mile from shore. While there was an incoming tide, and I had an inflatable life vest and the snorkel gear, I didn't think risking a swim of over a half mile was a good idea, especially dragging a tote bag loaded with clothing.

Indecision can kill a man at a time like this so I took a deep breath and went into action accelerating the boat and swinging wide to the port side of the target, and at the last moment turned the speedboat so it was perpendicular to the yacht. I braced myself, held the wheel with a death grip and pushed the throttle to its limit. The boat responded immediately. It was as nimble as a cougar chasing down his next meal. When the yacht was fifty yards distant I lit the fuse of the last remaining rocket, and the last of the remaining mortars that were surplus to my needs, and had not been used in the making of the rockets.

The fuses burned quickly and looked just like the sparklers kids play with. Only this wasn't playtime, this was for real. The rocket ignited with a whishing sound and flew accurately, on target, to the yacht's fiberglass hull. I knew the missile would not sink the yacht, but the exploding mortars in my boat, and the speedboat itself, would.

When the speedboat was thirty yards away from its target I abandoned ship. I sat on the railing and rolled off the railing backwards just as you see the scuba divers in the movies enter the water with tanks strapped to their back. But it didn't come off as well as the pro's do it. One of the flippers hooked on a deck cleat; it came off my foot and fell into the sea instantly sinking before I could retrieve it. *How the hell am I going make it back to shore with only one flipper? This is really bad luck. Another fine mess you got us into, Ollie.*

Putting the worrisome thought behind me for the moment I bobbed up and down in the water like a cork, and watched the speedboat race towards its target. I didn't want to miss a moment of the action.

It was going to be a sight to see; it was going to be too much fun to miss.

At the moment of contact, when the bowrider collided with the yacht, ten feet of hull disintegrated spewing white shreds of fiberglass into the air, both from my boat and its target. Simultaneously, when my boat impacted the yacht, the mortars exploded filling the air with an ear shattering noise, and the pyrotechnics were amazing. Red, white, orange and blue flames accentuated with sparkling bits of light filled the air. It was almost as impressive as the 4th Of July celebration held annually at the local beach back in Locust Valley. Francis Scott Key couldn't have been more impressed. I knew it was a bit of overkill, ramming the boat would have been sufficient to sink the yacht, but I wasn't taking any chances. And even if the explosions served no other purpose the intense bright light of the mortars and rocket would render the ship's crew temporarily blind, and the noise would leave them disorientated, hopefully giving me time to get the hell out of the area, and back into safe water.

While treading water, I watched for the yacht's occupants to leave the cabin and abandon ship. But suddenly I had another plan and it had better work because I didn't think I could make it ashore with only one flipper. However the plan depended on the number of survivors left on the boat. As luck had it, only one person left the cabin and he scrambled for safety. He was an older man about my age but obese, obviously out of shape. I surmised that he must be the "head honcho"; he was certainly not a drug runner. The old guy headed for the stern where a Zodiac, a rubberized boat often used as a lifeboat was secured. I watched him proceed aft, attentive to see if he was carrying a weapon, a gun or machine pistol. Lucky for me he was unarmed. All he carried was an attaché case. If he had a weapon I might have risked the long swim back to the beach. But since he was without a lethal weapon I decided to leave my sports bag behind. I left it floating in the water, and swam to the side of the boat adjacent to the transom where I would be out of the man's line of sight.

When I reached the stern still unobserved, and hidden from view, I watched as the man attempted to release the clamps securing the Zodiac. The yacht was settling into the sea rapidly, just moments from sinking, and the gunnels were awash in seawater. Finally, with a loud snap, the clamps released and the rubber boat came free of its bindings. The man threw his attaché case into the boat and prepared to step aboard.

At that instant I pushed off the transom with both feet using all the force I could muster, grabbed the Zodiac with both hands and kicked the water with the single flipper. The lifeboat was instantly propelled out into the sea. It coasted for a few yards before coming to rest, and floated gently in the calm water. I swam to the bow, grabbed the rope lifeline and proceeded to distance the Zodiac from the yacht.

When the lifeboat was roughly twenty feet away from the sinking ship I cautiously raised my head out of the water and looked back at the yacht to be sure a machine pistol was not facing me. If there was one I was prepared to dive and swim underwater to the safety of the night. But thank God the deck was empty. *But where is the old man? Is he in the water?*

What I did not realize while re-positioning the rubber boat was that the drug dealer had made it into the Zodiac. I looked up and saw him standing above me holding the aluminum attaché case high in the air. He was about to use it as a club to bash my head into pulp.

***

The moon had exited the cloud cover and its glow illuminated the aluminum case with an eerie light as it seemingly in slow motion came crashing down on my head. I instantly ducked into the water and the attaché case bounced harmlessly off the rubberized fabric. The force of the impact caused the boat to undulate in a harmonic motion sending the drug lord reeling sideways, and this gave me the opportunity to react. I reached up and grabbed the man's arm pulling him towards me before he could regain his footing and swing the case again. The case fell to the floorboards and the man fell forwards into the water and on top of me. Unfortunately he was above my body, his head out of the water, and I was in effect his life vest. I sank below the sea while he remained above it.

Somehow I managed to struggle to the surface gasping for air, barely making it before being out of breath. For the moment we were on equal footing, neither of us having the advantage. He must have been terrified. The fear was evident in his eyes; they were wide and unfocused. He ingested sea water and some of it must have entered his lungs because he began to choke and cough, and his panic sent a rush of adrenalin through his body giving him extraordinary strength. It was either that or I was weaker than I thought because he lunged forward and straddled my body like an octopus squeezing the life out of his prey, and I could not shake the man loose. Once again I sank under the water while he remained above it. The air in my lungs was running out. Years of smoking were taking its toll. There was only one thing left to do. My options were limited so I grabbed at his crotch and squeezed his genitals with all my strength. That did it; he let go and I managed to break free and somehow regained the surface. I gasped for air but also had the wits about me to act instinctively and push the Zodiac out of his reach before he regained his composure.

When the boat and I were safely out of harm's way I turned towards the man. He was clearly in trouble. I didn't think he knew how to swim, or the weight of his clothing was an anchor dragging him down because he thrashed about rising above and then sinking below the surface of the sea, all the while choking and coughing. I saw he was doomed but there was nothing I could do for him. Nor would

I have helped him, even if I wanted to, not even for a hefty profit. My mission was accomplished, and it was sufficient compensation.

***

After catching my breath I climbed aboard the little boat and watched as the man struggled to keep afloat. I viewed the unfolding scene without feeling compassion for the man, and without any emotion at all. When I was sure the man was doomed I tended to the motor. It only took one pull of the recoil cord to start the engine and it purred like a kitten. You have to admire the drug lords' attention to detail; they buy the best of everything and keep it in good shape. The shift lever slid easily into drive and I motored to the sports bag that floated gently in the water, and retrieved it. But I didn't immediately head back to shore. Instead I circled around to watch the man finally sink below the surface of the water for the last time. He was gone and I had no more feeling of remorse over his death than I would have had over a dead fish thrown back into the water. I was stoic as a stone. It was as if I had watched a movie as a spectator, not an active participant.

Before leaving the area, the killing zone, I scanned the water once more looking for evidence that might somehow incriminate me. There was none. There was no sign of the yacht, the drug dealers, or remains of the speedboat, or the contents therein. The yacht was gone, resting on the bottom, destined to become another artificial reef for divers to explore, and the denizens of the deep would consume the bodies. The sea holds many secrets that only King Neptune is privy to, and I hoped this incident would be one more of them.

Suddenly I became anxious to get out of the area for I feared the Coast Guard might be alerted by the sights and sounds of the fireworks and en route to the commotion, so I turned the boat east towards the shoreline and headed home. I didn't even think of the man I left to drown until a half hour later. And when I did think of him this time it was with a bit of compassion. I should have run the drug lord down with the Zodiac to put him out of his misery, or at least left him unconscious so he could die peacefully instead of drowning slowly and painfully. They say drowning is one of the worst ways to die. Water fills your lungs with a searing pain and you cough violently trying to expel the liquid, but to no avail.

After a few minutes Ollie's personality surfaced. "Oh well," I thought, "another meal for the lobsters and scavenging crabs, no big deal."

***

The incident had taken place about a half-mile offshore and roughly two miles south of the hotel, and I motored at a moderate speed to a public beach within walking distance of my temporary residence. Fortunately, at that late hour, it being after 1:00 AM, the beach was deserted and I anchored one hundred yards from the shore, in deep water, past the low tide line. When I sank the boat, I wanted to make sure it stayed undiscovered, at least until I was far away from Treasure Island.

The lifeboat had a survival kit, and included in the kit was a knife, and I used it to slash the several floatation compartments. The Zodiac whistled out air and quickly sank after burping a few last bubbles. I was alone in the water, just me, the attaché case and the tote bag. To the casual observer, if he happened to be out on the beach looking for shells, or on a late night stroll, I was just another vacationer taking a midnight dip before going to bed.

Carrying the sports bag in one hand and the attaché case in the other, I floated on my back and propelled myself to the shore using the single flipper. It was an easy swim and once ashore I buried the snorkel gear in the beach's dumpster under a foot of garbage, changed into street clothes and walked back to the hotel. It was roughly 2:00 AM when I entered the room. No one saw me and I saw no one. It was as if nothing had happened, a night like any other.

After showering I sat on the bed and prepared to open the locked attaché case. I was hoping to find incriminating evidence, records, transactions, names and addresses, and other information that could be forwarded to the police in the hope that they might use the knowledge in their pursuit of slowing down the drug trade in the St. Petersburg area. My work, the vigilante career, much as I enjoyed it was finished, or it would be once I got out of town. But that presented another problem. I couldn't retrieve my car. I could never go back to the marina without the rented boat, and even if I did somehow gain access to my SUV it would be of little use since the plates were stolen and there was probably an arrest warrant issued for me. No, I had to cut my losses and get out of town as soon as possible.

The motel room was an efficiency apartment with a kitchenette, a sink, a microwave oven and utensils sufficient for preparing small meals. This turned out to be very fortuitous because the kitchen cabinet had a heavy-duty corkscrew able to open almost anything. I used it to pry open the lock on the attaché case. What I saw amazed and delighted me. It was filled to the brim with one hundred dollar bills neatly stacked and neatly bound in ten thousand dollar bundles. A quick count showed there was well over a half million dollars. Who said crime doesn't pay?

***

I slept like a baby that night and if it was not for a ray of sunlight streaking through an opening of the heavy window drapery I might have slept till noon. After a quick hot shower and a couple of aspirin to ease the pain of the previous nights ordeal I packed my bag with the few clothes purchased the day before, the gold coins, the few remaining dollars I brought with me, and best of all, the contents of the attaché case. The shotgun was left behind, hidden under the bed. After a final last look around I called a local yellow cab and checked out of the motel. It was imperative to get the hell out of town as fast as possible, before the marina manager realized the rental speedboat was not moored safely at the dock.

Unfortunately I didn't have proper identification to fly Jet Blue, my favorite airline, or any airline for that matter, so my destination was the Greyhound bus station in Tampa. The lengthy trip probably made the cabby's entire day's pay but the cost was of little matter; I was wealthy, a millionaire.

***

After arriving at the bus terminal I booked the first bus headed for Texas. That would be my new home, a safe haven, a new life, and perhaps new and exciting adventures. Once I was settled I could secure bogus identification and a driver's license so it might be possible to open a bank account and buy a car. I had plenty of money to do whatever I wanted to do. As they say, "money talks, bullshit walks." You can do anything and buy anything as long as the money holds out.

While waiting for the bus that would take me to a new life I once again reflected on the things that had made me different from the person I once was. The night before I calmly and without remorse destroyed a house, killed two more people, and sank a boat without giving it a second thought. And I did it for the pure joy of the excitement. A year earlier I didn't have the guts to challenge a shopkeeper who might have inadvertently overcharged me a dollar at the checkout counter, and now I might beat the brains out of someone who cut me off at a traffic intersection. Who can figure? I was angry, surly and friendless immediately after the Ouija session, but now I am friendly, and sometimes compassionate, even when killing someone. After all, I'm not really such a bad person. I'm not sadistic or believe in torture. That's compassion, isn't it?

Can I blame my personality on the two entities coming to terms with each other, each of them compromising, giving in a little for the sake of harmony? I don't know. Life's a mystery, and there's no sense in trying to figure it all out. I'll just board the bus, take it as it comes, and do the best I can in my new home in Texas. But first I have to call my ex-landlord and have him look after Kitty.

Postscript

At one time or another we at times ask ourselves: "who am I, where am I going, and what comes next after the end of days?" Many of us also think about the circumstances that have made us who we are, and why we act the way we do. I often reflect about such things, perhaps excessively, but I think my obsessive musings are justified because I live in a twilight zone of the supernatural world not of my own choosing. I would rather be like everyone else, but it is not to be and I have to live with who I am.

The problem is that I can't control the occasional moments of precognition or telepathy. If I did, at least there would be some benefit, like winning the lottery. But a frustrating thing about the paranormal world is that the esoteric knowledge is capricious. I never know if revelations are real or just a put on to baffle me. An incident which might illustrate what I am talking about follows:

A few days ago (this actually was just a few days ago. I had just finished writing the last few pages of this book) I had a very compelling dream. I can't remember the details except that the numbers 1 and 3 stood out like a beacon of light. The memory was so strong that I could not get it out of my mind. And so I did what I have not done in years. I played the daily state lottery, the one that consists of only three numbers. Unfortunately I only had two numbers, and when I consulted with the lottery agent he told me to use a zero in place of the third number. And so I boxed in: 013, 301, 103, etc. Of course I lost. The numbers came in 113. If I boxed in only the two numbers I would have won.

I could go on and on telling stories about the supernatural world I live in, but I'm not Charles Dickens getting paid by the word count nor is this little novel *War and Peace*. However I would like to relate a few more incidences. The first one is not very compelling. In fact I'm sure most of you have had similar experiences. But I want to tell it because it may reveal how I got to be the person I am. It was my first out of body experience and to this day it is still one of the most vivid memories I have even though it took place almost seventy years ago.

My first out of body experience took place one night in the fall of the year, in October or perhaps November. Children don't pay much attention to days or months, not like those of us who are approaching the end of days. I remember it was cold and I had to wear a jacket when I went outside. The deciduous trees, the maples and oaks, were shedding their leaves, and I remember being fascinated with their many shades of gold and brown, and how the sun illuminated them as they floated in the air currents before finally coming to rest on the ground. But being fascinated by the falling leaves does not mean I was carefree or even happy. I was not. The upcoming winter was an unsettling and unhappy time for me.

We had just moved to a new neighborhood. I was in unfamiliar surroundings, in a new apartment and about to enter kindergarten in a few days. I don't know how my mother convinced the local school board to accept me at the tender age of four and a half since the school term had begun a month earlier, but mom had a certain way about her. She could convince anybody of anything. She never raised her voice or got excited or became argumentative when pursuing an unreasonable request, but somehow in the end she always won out and always got her way. And so I entered school early. This however was not necessarily a good thing. I was not ready for school. Not only was I the smallest kid in the class I was still very immature. It would have been better if my parents had enrolled me in a nursery school, but we never had that kind of money and pre-school was not free in those days.

Aside from the age handicap, and being small for my age, I was also the only Jew in the class. If you visited Flushing today you will find almost all the stores displaying Korean or Chinese signage but it is also a melting pot with Christians, Jews, Muslims and Buddhists living in harmony with each other. But in the 1940s, when we were fighting the enemy in Europe and in the Pacific the neighborhood was predominantly German (A few of them were Nazi sympathizing Jew haters) and Irish Catholics, and it was at a time before the Catholic Church officially exonerated the Jews for having killed Jesus, and I paid dearly for the Church's doctrines.

My memories of elementary school were of having to endure taunts of "Christ killer", and having to run home from school before the Irish kids intercepted me. Occasionally the kids ran faster than I, and I suffered for it. And so it was that for the first few years in school I was a loner and escaped the realities of everyday life by looking inward to a fantasy world of my own creation.

But I'm getting ahead of myself. I get sidetracked very easily. It's just that my early school days are an indelible scar on my life and I can't help reliving them. Maybe if I verbalize the pain enough it will eventually be expunged from my mind.

To get back to the out of body experience, it happened on the day we moved to Bowne Street in Flushing N.Y. We had previously lived in the rear apartment of a two family house, and I had to adjust to living in a large building full of strangers, and find the courage to enter an elevator, a frightening enclosed cage that transported me to our apartment three stories above the street. But the most unsettling thought was that our new home was far from my cousins, the relatives I knew, and the people I was comfortable with. I was unprepared to make new friends and never learned how to form relationships with other kids as I had never gone to a play group, or even to a nursery school. My parents had neither the time nor the money for what they thought was foolishness. But in my parents defense I have to admit that they never had to cope with a new environment having lived in Brooklyn, NY, in what was in effect a *de facto* Jewish ghetto where everyone supported each other, and where they were insulated from a hostile world. So they never knew the fear and isolation I felt, and why I dreaded going to school. I was frightened at the thought of meeting new people and having to make new friends. I was one very unhappy little boy.

On the first night in our new home I suppose I played with a few toys after dinner and then sent off to bed without a word of reassurance or comfort. For my parents it was just a night like any other. For me it was traumatic. I can't blame them for not knowing how scared I was. But maybe they should have known, and sat with me for a little while in my bedroom, and perhaps read a bedtime story until I fell asleep. But they didn't, and it's all water under the bridge now, or is it?

I lay in bed thinking I would never fall asleep. My eyes were shut tight the better to keep the monsters locked away in the closet. I remember that I was still awake when my parents had retired for the night and the house was still and quiet except for the hissing of the steam radiator under the window sill. But I finally dozed off and soon entered into a deep dreamless sleep. Sometime during the night I awoke, slowly at first, then becoming conscious, in small increments, until my eyes were wide open and I was fully awake. After a moment or two I looked up and saw the ceiling light descending from the ceiling, coming closer and closer to my body. For a moment I thought the fixture had come loose from the ceiling and was slowly falling towards me. But I wasn't fearful that it would crash into my body and injure me. It was moving too slowly for that to happen.

After a few moments, when I realized I would not be hurt, I turned my head and looked downward towards the bed. There I was, sleeping peacefully under the fuzzy covers. I looked back up to the ceiling. The light fixture was not falling; I was floating upwards towards the ceiling. I stopped halfway between the bed and the ceiling for a moment and surveyed the room. There was nothing amiss. A light streamed through the partially opened window, and I looked towards it. My dad had not yet installed blinds or shades and the moon shone brightly in a cloudless sky illuminating the room with an eerie glow. The moon as seen through the widow seemed to summon me and I floated towards it and passed through the glass effortlessly, as though it was not glass at all but a heliographic illusion. I was a spirit having form but no substance and once outside the building felt neither the cold nor the wind of the autumn night.

When I left the building I looked down into the road three floors below. The streetlights illuminated the street, now empty except for parked cars. The darkened apartment houses, the barren trees, and the trees that were still shedding their leaves, came into view, and I floated in mid air above it all. After orientating myself to the surroundings I headed south and traveled for several hundred yards up the street towards the old neighborhood.

Suddenly a frightening thought burst into my mind. It was the realization that I could not go to our former home. My parents were sleeping in the new apartment not the old one. The old neighborhood was gone forever; I could not go back, not now, not ever. Reluctantly, I turned around and like a feather held aloft by the slightest current of air, floated back to the warmth of my bed. But the journey back home was not without incident. As I approached our apartment I saw a maple leaf caught in a gust of wind rising upwards to the sky. The leaf fascinated me and I approached it with an open hand hoping to retrieve it. But as I reached for the leaf it moved away from my fingers as if a force propelled it forward just out of reach. It was as if my hand and the leaf were polarized with a magnetic charge repelling each other. The leaf continued to travel in front of me, gently floating a few inches in front of my outstretched hand. After an undetermined time, a few minutes or perhaps just a few seconds, I noticed that I had arrived home and I passed through the solid portion of the bedroom window as easily as a beam of light, and the floating maple leaf passed through the partially opened window.

The next morning I awoke refreshed, the memory of the previous night crystal clear and vivid in my mind. I realized that I was no longer unsettled and afraid. The experience had served to alley my fears and anxieties over the relocation. I accepted the fact that the life back in our old apartment was a thing of the past and I was ready to face new challenges, make new friends and move on.

When I got out of bed the first thing I did was to look for the maple leaf and there it was, on the floor, in front of the window.

***

Dreams are fleeting moments in time and soon forgotten, but this experience is something I will never forget. It is a memory as vivid today as it was so many years ago. It was no dream.

I know the out of body experience as described is not a very compelling story, but I wanted to mention it as it was the first of many paranormal happenings. Most of you will dismiss the tale as a dream because what goes on in your head cannot be verified. There is no real evidence except for a fallen leaf. Maybe if I flew down to the street and picked up a rock or a piece of paper, and brought it back home with me, and woke up in the morning holding the evidence the tale might be more credible. But a spirit cannot pick up anything. He might be able to move things around using an energy force, but picking up things? I don't think so.

**

One incident that comes to mind of a spirit using energy to move objects took place much later, when I was an adult. It's not an earth-shattering story but I like to tell it anyway.

Susan and I wed shortly before I was deployed to Germany, to a small airbase located in the foothills of the Eiffel Mountains. While most airman leave their brides back home with their family I was so desperately in love that I couldn't leave my new wife behind, so she joined me as soon as I got settled in. However the military discourages enlisted personnel from bringing their families with them when they are stationed overseas, and for that reason I was denied base housing. With my meager salary I had no other choice than to rent a small apartment over a barn, in a farming village ten miles from the base. We were in the wilderness, separated from the normal comforts and benefits that living on the base would have provided. We were foreigners in a strange land, emigrants as our grandparents were when they came to the United States through Ellis Island.

Life was not easy, and only newlyweds who were in love would tolerate the conditions we lived in. Susan awoke before me every day and made a fire in the kitchen coal stove to heat the apartment. She cooked our meals on the same stove, and then washed the dishes in a sink with only one tap, a cold-water tap. We didn't have a refrigerator either, so Susan had to shop daily and we ate whatever the butcher slaughtered that day. If he slaughtered a pig we ate pork. We ate horsemeat on more than one occasion. Our one luxury was a coal fired bath tub, but it took all day to heat up enough water for one tubful of hot water, so we had to bathe together, and it was on a Saturday night. But I digress; I tend to do that a lot. I get distracted easily.

The Telekinetic incident concerns an antique clock that was given to be by my next-door neighbor while living in the German farming village. He was a pensioner, a disabled veteran who had lost a leg and an eye while fighting the Russians on the Eastern Front. Since he couldn't work the farm he had a lot of time on his hands, and we filled some of it playing chess. We became fast friends and when it became time for me to return to the states he gave me his most prized possession, an old ornamental clock which had been in his family for several generations. The clock contained a bright copper pendulum and a glass dome covering visible mechanical gears. It also had an alarm feature, although the alarm did not work.

Several years passed. I had completed four years of military service, was discharged from the Air Force, and living back home in New York working towards a degree in business administration.

Before enlisting I previously attended a state university but dropped out after a semester due to lack of funds. As a veteran however, and with the GI Bill providing a nice stipend of $135.00 a month, it was possible for me to be a full time student at Hunter College while Susan worked as a secretary for a manufacturing company in Long Island City. Things were tight but we were able to afford a basement apartment in Jackson Heights. It wasn't much, but still better than living with one of our parents.

The incident happened on a Saturday. Susan and I and another couple, Bob and Sara, close friends since high school had spent the day at Jones Beach State Park. It's on the ocean and a great place to swim and relax on the sandy beach. Afterwards, after a shower and a change of clothes we had plans to meet our friends for dinner.

We got home from the beach about 3:00 PM, showered and reclined on the bed to rest for a few minutes. I remember saying to Susan, "don't fall asleep; we have to get ready soon. We have to be dressed and out of here by 5:30 for our dinner date with Bob and Sara". But the sun and the surf took its toll; we both fell fast asleep.

Suddenly we were startled, and awoke to the chime of an alarm clock. Strange, I thought, our alarm clock has a buzzer not a chime, and I went to the bedroom dresser to shut off the alarm. But it was not the alarm clock that was ringing. I followed the chime, and it led me to the living room, to the clock my German friend had given me. It was the source of the sound. I turned it off and looked at the time. The hour hand was set at 10 and the minute hand at 30. Not that it mattered though, the clock had stopped running soon after we returned home from overseas, and it was just a decorative piece we kept as a souvenir, a small reminder of our deployment in Europe. I returned to the bedroom and looked at my watch. It was a few minutes after 5:00 PM. We had just enough time to get dressed and get out of the house by 5:30 PM.

When we met our friends for dinner, and while seated at the restaurant I relayed the incident over a glass of wine. Bob said "Yeah, sure, and tell me another one". He didn't believe a word I said. Oh, by the way, nothing happened that night, but I wonder what might have happened if we didn't wake up. Would we have been killed in a car accident while speeding to our dinner date?

Telekinesis harnesses the mind's energy to move inanimate objects, often through concentration. But it never works for me through concentration. Telekinetic movement only occurs when I am not fully awake, or alert, or in a semi-somnolent state. I cannot control inanimate objects using conscious thought, but only through my sub-conscious mind, and when I least expect it.

***

I believe that all humans have an internal spirit or a foreign entity that occasionally influences us or makes itself known to us when we least expect it. An example you might relate to is *Déjà vu*.

We all have had at one time or another *Déjà vu* or precognitive experiences. How often have you been someplace for the very first time, somewhere you have never been before, but you feel that the surroundings are familiar? Let's suppose you are dining out while on vacation. You have never been to this city, and you are not in a franchised cookie cutter restaurant. The restaurant is unique, perhaps one that serves Sushi, and you have never been to a Sushi restaurant. You are seated at a table by the window and you know you have sat at that table before. You look towards your left and there are people seated at an adjoining table, and they look familiar although you have never met them. The waiter comes over and takes your order and you know you have ordered that particular meal once before, even though you have not. You talk to your companion and suddenly feel you are talking about a subject you have once previously discussed. This is precognition and I defy you to tell me that you have not experienced it at least once in your life. But I have deja vu experiences all the time. And they are more than just thinking I have seen or heard something before.

***

While Déjà Vu is a powerful feeling of having experienced an event that took place in the past while precognition or clairvoyance is looking into the future. I can relate a typical precognition incident that will demonstrate what I am trying to explain.

Susan and I have a ritual we observe every day. She finishes her work (our office is in our home) at 4:00 PM and joins me in the bedroom with a glass of Zinfandel for herself and a glass of red wine for me. Meanwhile I retrieve from our bedroom refrigerator a packet of cheese, Munster for her, and Swiss for myself. We then lounge on the bed and turn on Judge Judy, the TV judge, and watch the show while munching on cheese and drinking wine.

I think the fascination of the show is that we see other people with more problems than we have. Sort of makes you feel superior. At 5:00 PM when the episode ends Susan goes to the kitchen and prepares the evening meal, and I take a nap. After I awake from my nap and before I leave the bedroom for dinner I always tune the TV to the movie guide to see what was programmed for that evening.

On one recent occasion while eating dinner I said to Susan, "There's a good movie I saw on the guide and I'd like to see it tonight. It's a Clint Eastwood movie, *The Unforgiven*, and it's on at eight o'clock." She said, "Sure, there's nothing in particular I want to see." But when we sat down to watch TV later that evening the movie was not listed on any channel for that day. However when I checked the TV guide the following week it was aired on the channel I saw listed in the movie guide the previous week, and at 8:00 PM, the same time slot.

Incidences like this are not earth shattering. I never see tragic incidences: airplanes engulfed in flames plummeting to earth, or horrific murders, or devastating earthquakes, or any tragedy coming to pass. Nevertheless, I sometimes see into the future and it's only when I am not fully in control of my senses. I have the visions when I am dozing off or just awaking, when my spirit is not confined by the conservative thoughts that society imposes on my mind.

***

Considering all the paranormal experiences I have experienced, and considering what others have told me has led to the conclusion that all of us, all human beings, have a spiritual connection to a place that exists outside our physical world. If we ignore the ridicule of the skeptic, and opened our minds to what is possible, a world would open for us that only a few people understand. Unfortunately the majority of civilized people are constrained by a lifetime of cultural conditioning, and it has alienated us from our inner self and our soul. But fortunately there are still enough of us who keep the candle of esoteric knowledge burning. We believe in the paranormal and because we do believe other dimensions exist, they open their doors to us. I have met people who have the uncanny gift of seeing the ghostly aura that surrounds our bodies. Could this luminescent aura be an ethereal spirit from another dimension, a soul that lives within us? Is the entity a spirit that was born when we were born, and will die when we die? Or are our unseen spirits eternal, living within our body while we live, and passed on to another human form when we have taken our last breath?

I think the answer in part can be found in Carl Jung's (The father of analytical psychology) writings. His theory of the "Collective Unconscious" touches on the subject. He believed that we have an unseen linkage, one soul to another, and of our connection to a higher order of intelligence. He wrote:

"My thesis then, is as follows: in addition to our immediate consciousness, which is of a thoroughly personal nature and which we believe to be the only empirical psyche (even if we tack on the personal unconscious as an appendix), there exists a second psychic system of a collective, universal, and impersonal nature which is identical in all individuals. This collective unconscious does not develop individually but is inherited. It consists of pre-existent forms, the archetypes, which can only become conscious secondarily and which give definite form to certain psychic contents".

CG Jung, The Archetypes and the Collective Unconscious

Cark Jung's theories may have been influenced by Albert Einstein's work. They were friends and met to discus their work over a series of dinners between 1909 and 1912. Jung later wrote "It was Einstein who first started me thinking about a relativity of time as well as space, and their psychic conditionality". Einstein at the time was working on and solidifying his postulations on "The Universal Theory of everything".

The "Universal Theory of Everything" is a scientifically accepted expression. Einstein called it the "Unified Field Theory", but no matter, whatever words we choose, it's the theory that explains everything.

Einstein believed that the field is the unification of space and time into what is now called the time-space continuum. The theory replaces Euclid's three-dimensional world with another dimension, the fourth dimension, that of time. If we accept Einstein's postulations then what may already has happened in the future, and what took place in the past, are no less real than what we experience in the here and now. And if we extrapolate the idea of a fourth dimension then there is the possibility that unseen entities might exist in a universe where time and space is irrelevant.

Resources

The following is a partial list of resources I drew upon in the writing of this book. You may find the information contained in the following books and websites interesting and informative, and a stepping stone for further research into the subject of the paranormal.

Institute of Noetic Sciences - www.noetic.org

This website was founded by Edgar Mitchell, an astronaut on Apollo 14. Mitchell founded the IONS institute in 1973. An excerpt from the website follows:

"The Institute has systematically investigated the nature of consciousness with scientific rigor and from numerous perspectives, contributing to an ongoing paradigm shift that recognizes the essential role consciousness plays in our human evolution.

Significant projects conducted or supported during IONS' formative years include:

1. Research on mind-body interactions, healing, psycho-neuroimmunology, and spontaneous remission, bioenergetics, and the nature of the "healing response".

2. Laboratory studies consisting of extended human capacities, including precognition, gut feelings, extrasensory perception, and remote viewing.

3.   Anthropological fieldwork on dream sharing in the Amazon and on claims of reincarnation around the world.
4.   systematic analysis of the core metaphysical assumptions underlying the dominant model of reality"

Dr. Randolph Byrd - examined the power of prayer. His research seems to indicate that prayer does work. The following article is taken from one of his papers:

"Positive therapeutic effects of intercessory prayer in a coronary care unit population" Southern Medical Journal 1988 July; 81(7): 826-9 abstract: Over ten months, 393 patients admitted to the CCU were randomized, after signing informed consent, to an intercessory prayer group (192 patients) or to a control group (201 patients). While hospitalized, the first group received IP by participating Christians praying outside the hospital; the control group did not. At entry, chi-square and stepwise logistic analysis revealed no statistical difference between the groups. After entry, all patients had follow-up for the remainder of the admission. The IP group subsequently had a significantly lower severity score based on the hospital course after entry (P less than .01). Multivariant analysis separated the groups on the basis of the outcome variables (P less than .0001). The control patients required ventilatory assistance, antibiotics, and diuretics more frequently than patients in the IP group. These data suggest that intercessory prayer to the Judeo-Christian God has a beneficial therapeutic effect in patients admitted to a CCU.

Edgar Cayce, the Sleeping Prophet, is my favorite seer because his secretary documented all of his predications and readings while under hypnosis... Cayce is most famous for health readings given remotely to patients while under a hypnotic state. Many consider him the father of holistic medicine. His foundation is still active. You can visit the website at **www.edgarcayce.org**

Peter Hurkos www.peterhurkos.com

The following is an excerpt from the website:

"Peter Hurkos is considered by experts to have been the world's foremost psychic. Born May 21, 1911, in Dordrecht, Holland died June 1, 1988 He acquired his psychic gift in 1941 after falling from a ladder and suffering a brain injury. He was in a coma for three days at the Zuidwal Hospital. Upon regaining consciousness, he discovered that he had developed an ability to pierce the barriers that separate the past, present and the future.

In 1956, Hurkos was brought to the United States to be tested at his Glen Cove, Maine medical research laboratory. For two-and-a-half years he was tested under tightly controlled conditions. The results convinced Dr. Puharich that Hurkos' psychic abilities were far greater than any he had ever tested, a remarkable 90% accuracy.

Decorated as a war hero by Queen Juliana of The Netherlands, he had been a consultant to every President of the United States from Eisenhower to Reagan. Hurkos received countless police badges from police chiefs around the world, including one from the International Police Association, and Interpol. His Holiness, Pope Pius XII, decorated Hurkos stating; "I hope you will always use your God-given Gift for the betterment of mankind. Use it as an instrument to touch the people, to help them."

Ian Stevenson, MD – Author of: *Children who remember previous lives, a question of reincarnation*
The University press of Virginia 1992
The book is entirely objective and perhaps the best validation of reincarnation. In his book Dr. Stevenson documents 12 cases of children who believe they have lived a life before their current incarnation.

JB Rhine - Duke University Durham NC. - was a scientist employed by Duke University to research paranormal activity.
J.B. Rhine investigated ghosts, telepathy, poltergeists, and other unseen parapsychology phenomena from 1927 to 1965 at his Duke laboratory.
Duke magazine Volume 95, No.6, November 2009

Ervin Laszlo - a respected Quantum scientist is quoted as saying:

"This (Quantum Vacuum) is a super dense cosmic frictionless medium that carries all the universal forces of nature", and a "sea of information conveying the historical experience of matter."

Max Planck – German physicist (1858-1947) originated the quantum theory stated that:

"All matter originates and exists only by virtue of a force... We must assume behind this force the existence of a conscious and intelligent Mind. This Mind is the matrix of all matter."

Conclusion

The above list of resources is by no means a complete compilation of reference material but they are the most compelling. Seers and prognosticators such as Nostradamus have been omitted as their predications make for an interesting read, but are too vague to be considered as a verifiable source of information.

Spiritual text as found in the teachings of Buddhism and Hinduism provide us with a moral compass and speak of reincarnation and the Akashic records, but once again they offer no documented proof of the spiritual world.

I suppose it all comes down to a matter of faith, whether to believe that there is something to look forward to after we are gone from the earth, or not.

But I will always remember what my philosophy teacher once told me when I questioned the existence of God. He said, "The atheist will never have the satisfaction of saying, "I told you so."

Author Biography

In this, his first full length book, *The Ouija Board Killer*, Donald Macnow has drawn upon a lifetime of what he calls, "living on the edge of the paranormal universe."

The autographical novel recounts many of his esoteric life experiences woven into a tale of demonic possession, madness and murder. Excerpts from the novel and a discussion forum can be found at his website, TheOuija.net and at his blog, TheOuijaSpeaks.blogspot.com

Mr. Macnow's latest short story, "Fire-Fight on the Road to Tal-Afar", is included in the Scribes Valley Publishing Company's annual writing contest. The anthology is due to be published in 2012.

Donald has recently retired and currently lives in Glen Cove, NY with his wife Georgie. His interests include tennis, antique cars, and writing while his wife keeps busy managing the family business.

They are empty nesters sharing their home with a hyperactive Siamese cat named Digger.

Made in the USA
Charleston, SC
20 January 2014